⚡JOHNNY⚡
ASTRONAUT

RORY CARMICHAEL

Jodene & Larry —

Hope you enjoy & I hope to see you soon! (in NYC!!!)

This is a work of fiction. All of the characters and events portrayed in this book are either products of the author's twisted imagination or are used ficticiously.

Johnny Astronaut

Copyright© 2004 by Jeffrey Dinsmore

All rights reserved, including the right to reproduce this book, or portions thereof, in any form.

Cover art by Dennis Hayes

A Contemporary Press Book
Published by Contemporary Press
Brooklyn, New York

www.contemporarypress.com

ISBN 0-9744614-3-1

First edition: February 2004

Printed in the United States of America

Liner Notes

These people I can tolerate – Bello Lamb, Denise Betts, Bigbooté, Josh and Ginny Biggs, Don Brewer, Michael Birch and Bricken Meyer, Marc Brody, Oliver Butler, Richard Butt and Molly Gilmore, Chris and Devon Cassidy, the Dead Milkmen, Kessa de Santis, Brian and Alison Fairweather, Aileen Feeney, Lisi Grewe, Anne Harris, John Heberer, Maria Howes, Kyle Jarrow, Jill and Joe Kleinbriel, Valerie Krasny, Matt and Wendy Lilya, Merideth Lindeman, Lisa Magnus, Sydney Maresca, Marvin the Martian, Jon McCarron, Peter McGouran, Rick Meril, Bethann Miale, the Muskegonites, Devin T. Quin, Pixies, Matt and Sarah Ransford, Dave Ratzlow, Jeff Rosenberg, Samuel Sadden, Jesse Schiffrin, Jennifer Suhayda, Vic Thrill, We Are Scientists, Abby and Phil Young, Louise Zervas, 1st Hayden, 403 Church

These people I actually sort of like – Babe: Pig in the City, Dr. Sasha Brody, Travis Chamberlain, Roald Dahl, the Daniels, Amanda Dinsmore, Bob and Florence Dinsmore, Eileen and Dennis Dinsmore, the Gornickis, Laurie Loosey, Mary Ellen McGonnagal, Declan McManus, Peg and Maynard Owen, Sue Sharley, Carolyn Swosinski, Becky Yamamoto

These people should rest in peace – Justin Owen, Betty Sharley

These people should be set on fire and have their ashes run through a cheese grater – Jay Brida, Jeffrey D., Jess Dukes, Dennis Hayes, Jennifer Lilya, Charles Nickles, Chris Reese, Mike Segretto, the Sifter, the Little Sailor Boy, You

To read more of my stupid bullshit, visit
www.needlesonthebeach.com

JOHNNY ASTRONAUT

RORY CARMICHAEL

2

"Next stop, Outer Borzoi."

I was on a shuttle returning from Aquari with 50 large burning a hole in my pocket so deep I could feel the flames on my toenails. Back on Aquari, I had run into a little trouble with a nasty bunch of Ptsaurians who had hired me to find their dead uncle. Turned out the dead uncle was neither dead nor an uncle. Ptsaurians, I discovered, were not the most tolerant race of people when it came to crises of sexual identity. Luckily, I managed to hot-foot it out of there just before the dirty stuff hit the fan, leaving the Ptsaurians and their new aunt to work out their family issues among themselves. Something told me their formerly dead uncle would soon be stepping back into the grave for good.

But what happened on Aquari stayed on Aquari. I had bigger concerns at the moment; namely, the future existence of my livelihood. That weasel Charvez from Central Development had sent me a telegram while on Aquari; seemed the papers had finally come in and my office would be shut down if I didn't pay off a considerable sum in fines post-haste. Shame, because I had planned to donate that 50 large to help feed the ponies at Clinton Downs.

The shuttle pulled into the docking station, and I bolted out of my seat, first in line at the door. The stewardess threw me a sheepish grin through plastic teeth. Any other day, I might have taken her aside and given her the treatment, but it was getting late and I had bills to pay.

I ran out of the shuttle and past the suckers at the baggage claim. When you live on the edge like I do, you learn to pack light.

As I was exiting the docking station, a familiar set of gams was entering. I never forget a leg, especially when it comes with a twin.

"Well, well, well. If it isn't Johnny Astronaut," came a voice from somewhere above the legs.

I looked up into the face of Martha Vanderpool, an old friend. I use the word "friend" loosely. A better word might be "enemy."

"I thought slumming it had gone out of vogue," she sneered.

"Go suck a lemon," I replied, at a loss for anything better. Martha had that affect on me. Could be worse, I thought. She could still be my wife.

"What's the matter, Johnny?" she purred through a crocodile grin. "Mean old Mr. Charvez still trying to shut the place down? You needn't worry about it, Johnny. I've just come from your office. Everything's paid up proper."

She was a hell of a dame, all right. Paying off my fines with money she'd stolen from me. A real humanitarian.

"What do you want from me?" I asked.

"How about you and me get a drink and we discuss this like civilized human beings?" she offered.

I weighed my options. Take the free rent and whatever was

behind door number three, or pay the rent myself and lose a week's worth of gambling funds. I may have been down on my luck, but I wasn't stupid. I had a monkey, and the track didn't take good intentions.

We slid into a vinyl booth at Calcutta's, a joint I frequented just across the way from the docking station. To a casual observer, Martha, with her fashionable designer outfit and expensive shoes, would have looked out of place among the smugglers, prostitutes, and hopheads who frequented the watering hole. I was not a casual observer. Calcutta's was the kind of place that was tailor-made for a chick like Martha—loud, brash, and thoroughly obnoxious.

I ordered two Old-Fashioneds for myself and nothing for Martha. She didn't seem to take offense.

"I need you to find out some information for me," she said, helping herself to one of my drinks.

"Everyone wants information," I said, "and no one wants to give it. What's in it for me?"

"Listen, jerk," she said, "if it weren't for me, you'd be conducting your business affairs out of a cardboard box. The least you can do is hear me out."

"Nice, Martha," I answered. "Only next time you decide to do me a favor, do me a favor and don't do me any favors."

"Noted. Now shut up and let me tell you how you can help."

Over the next few rounds, (or possibly the next few), Martha explained the whole seedy story to me. The week before, she had run into an old friend of ours, Guy Febreezi of the Bontemps

Febreezis. The Febreezis, as anyone from Bontemps knew, were the family to talk to when you needed something done cheap. And when I say something, I mean anything. The Febreezis had their hands in the pockets of every service business in Outer Borzoi, from shuttle repair to fast food to plumbing. You needed a ride to the airport or you needed to buy a carton of smokes, it didn't matter; somewhere along the line, your money would be handled by the Febreezis. Usually right at the end.

"Guy has this new business proposal; a real honey of a deal," Martha continued, clutching a cigarette between her teeth. "Says it's going to make the Febreezis legit. He needs an investor, so he asked me to pony up some cash. I want you to look into the deal and tell me if it's worth my time."

I swirled the remains of my drink around in the glass. "Something doesn't add up," I said. "Why would Guy Febreezi need to borrow from you? He's got plenty of dough and plenty of ways to get more."

"He wants all of the money in this deal to come in aboveboard. Says he wants to turn over a new leaf."

I grimaced. "The only leaves that guy's turning over are the kinds that grow on a money tree."

"That was poor," she said.

"Whaddya want from me?" I asked. "I'm soused."

3

I woke up the next morning feeling like someone had bashed me in the head with a two-by-four. Immediately thereafter, someone bashed me in the head with a two-by-four.

I came to on the davenport in my living room. My head ached like a country song. Some 350-pound gorilla sat in my easy chair, watching a terrible old Karen Jamey movie on the telescreen.

He turned his fat head toward me. "Howaya, Astronaut?" he asked. "Ya' seem a little sore."

"Not nearly as sore as you're gonna be when you get to the end of this movie," I said. "Here's a hint: Jamey dies."

"Thanks for ruining it for me, Astronaut," he sneered. "Now I'm gonna have to ask for a refund."

He turned his attention back to the set. I slowly raised myself up into a sitting position. Pain shot through my head like a fat kid on a water slide. I grabbed a half-empty pack of Palmettos from the coffee table and lit one up. The smoke did nothing to help my headache.

"Do you mind if I ask what you're doing here?" I asked, whether he minded or not.

He turned back to me, annoyed.

"Febreezi," he said.

"Febreezi," I answered.

"Febreezi," he said.

"You know any other words?" I asked.

"Yeah, smart-ass," he replied. "I know some other words. Heard a few good ones on the street lately. Heard that you've been sticking your head in a few places that it shouldn't be. If you know what's good for ya', you'll mind your business and let your wife handle hers."

"First of all," I explained through a freshly exhaled plume of smoke, "she's my ex-wife. Second of all, what kind of manners did your mother teach you? When you bash a guy in the face with a piece of wood, it's common courtesy to introduce yourself."

"Ya' wanna know my name, Astronaut?" the Ape asked. He then lowered the footrest, stood up, and smashed a boot through my telescreen. The screen sputtered and sparked like an electronic firecracker.

"That's my name. Now stop sticking your beak in other people's honey. Ya' got me?"

He lumbered across the living room and paused with his hand on the doorknob.

"Oh, and one more thing, Astronaut," he said, "get yourself some rest. You look like hell."

He turned the knob and walked out of the apartment. I stared at the crackling telescreen and thought about what I was going to eat for breakfast.

Charvez from Central Development had been kind enough to let himself into my office and stink the place up for my arrival. When I walked in, he was sitting in the waiting room, flipping through the latest issue of *Postmodern Detective*. I hung my coat up on the rack and poured myself a cup of week-old coffee.

"Your ex-wife really helped you out of a jam last night, Astronaut," Charvez said. "Why do you want to get yourself wrapped up in another one?"

I sipped my coffee and pretended he wasn't there. Now if only I could get him to pretend it, too.

"I don't understand you, Astronaut," he continued. "You manage to carve yourself a hot piece of chicken like that and then you let her fly the coop. If I were you, I'd be in bed with her right now, making her feel dirty."

"Instead, you're you, and you're in my office, and you're making me feel dirty," I sneered. "You got your money, Charvez. Now why don't you get yourself lost?"

"Guess I got an internal compass, Astronaut. Always points to garbage."

"So you spend all day following your breath around, huh?"

As if to prove my point, Charvez yawned, spewing more of his toxic odor into the air.

"I'm gonna get out of here, Astronaut, if that's what you want. But let me make one thing clear to you; pull another one of those jobs like you did in July, and you're mine. And if you're mine, you're Central Development's. And if you're Central Development's, you're International Security's, and you do not want to be International Security's, Astronaut. You used your Get Out of Jail Free card; next time, you're not going to be so lucky."

He ripped a page out of my magazine, crumbled it into a ball, and threw it on the ground in a terrifying show of power. I didn't have the heart to tell him I had another copy at home.

I didn't like to admit it, but Charvez did have a lot of power over me. As a Surveillance Officer for Central Development, his job was to keep an eye on people like me and make sure that all was on the up-and-up. Translation: his job was to make sure that Central D. got their piece of the profit. Ever since Charvez took over the local post, it has been increasingly difficult for guys like me to bend the law. Guys like Febreezi, no problem. They just cut Central D. into the action and go about their business. Things aren't so simple for those of us on the bottom. I have a hard enough time cutting myself in on the action, let alone Charvez and the rest of the goons down at Central D.

"I used to have a guy like you in my regiment back during the lode wars on Tarmac," Charvez blabbered on.

"Are you still here?" I asked.

"All right, I'm gone," Charvez said. "But you be on your best behavior, Astronaut. Remember, the walls have eyes."

He hoofed it out of my office, slamming the door behind him.

"Good riddance," I muttered. Guy like Charvez'll make ya' mutter.

I sat down at my desk and thought back on the last two days. Something smelled funny. I'd known Martha for many years, been married to her for many more, and trusted her for many less. Martha was the kind of girl who would turn on a rattlesnake for the right price. I didn't think for one second that this Febreezi business was above the board ... a guy whacks you in the face with a two-by-four, and you start to get a pretty clear picture of things after the fuzziness goes away.

But it was a mystery, and I was the kind of guy who was a sucker for a mystery. I had to get to the bottom of it, not to help out Martha, but to satisfy my curiosity. Sometimes, you pull a little string and you can unravel the whole sweater. I just needed to find the right string.

4

Later that afternoon, I paid a visit to Guy Febreezi over at his factory in Bontemps, the industrial center of Outer Borzoi. From the outside, the place looked like another of the many nondescript Bontemps factories—smoke spewing from the roof, trucks driving in and out, a parking lot full of cars. Step through the doors, though, and you got a different picture. Where one might expect to find industrial machinery or stored goods, one found instead a lavish casino, filled with blank-eyed zombies and some of the shadiest characters in the Outer Borzoi underworld. My palms itched at the sight of it, the kind of itch that can only be scratched by the smooth surface of a hand of poker cards.

Much as I wanted to throw my money away, I had bigger business to attend to. Somewhere in the building, Guy Febreezi was plotting his latest business move, and I wanted to be in on the cut. Before I could talk to him, however, I had to get past the Remolian in the doorway with the laser pistol pointed at me.

"What's yer hurry, bub?" he asked me in a tiny pipsqueak

voice. I had smoked cigars that were bigger than this guy, and I've smoked some pretty small cigars.

"My hurry is my worry," I answered. "Now why don't you put that big ol' gun away and let me take a look around?"

He fired a shot from his laser pistol that came so close to my ear I could hear it singing. The laser pistol may have been small, but its beam was still deadly.

"I'm gonna ask you again," he squeaked. "What's yer hurry, bub?"

"You might wanna watch that, pal," I said. "I don't know if Mr. Febreezi would like you killing one of his best customers."

"I ain't never seen you in here before," the Remolian said. "And I seen everyone. Now why don't you make like a stripper and shake it?"

"Tell ya' what, friend," I said, "howsabout you get on your little communicator there and tell Febreezi that Johnny Astronaut is here to see him?"

The Remolian picked up his communicator. I heard him speaking in hushed tones to the person on the other end. After a minute or so of back and forth, he set the communicator down and put his laser pistol back in its tiny holster.

"All right, Astronaut, yer clear," he said. "But get this straight—I don't like you."

"Aw, that's I shame," I replied, as I strolled past him. "I was gonna ask you to the prom."

I left the slug behind and walked down the front stairs, onto the casino floor. The enormity of the building was accentuated by the gigantic mirrors covering the walls. To my left were the gaming tables. This was where the high rollers congregated to piss away the money they made from beating down the common man. The tables were all being watched over by Remolians. Remolians made good employees because they lacked the ability to lie. They made lousy employees because they could easily be squashed like bugs by pissed-off gamblers.

To the left were the slots. Next to the pony races, slots were my biggest bugaboo. The people seated at the machines all had a similar glassy-eyed look about them, as though somewhere, there was something they were supposed to do but were ignoring. Slots weren't like the table games; those actually required a modicum of skill and attention. I knew what it was like to sit in front of a machine and wake up ten hours later with no money or drive. From my eye, the slots alone had to be bringing in half a mil a day. Why would Febreezi wanna go clean when he was making this much cash dirty?

It took everything in my power to make it all the way across the floor and to the office without spending a single dime. When I saw who was guarding the office door, I wanted to turn around and do the walk again. The 350-pound ape who had bashed me with the two-by-four was standing next to the door with a smile on his face the size of China. At least, I assumed it was supposed to be a smile ... his lips were open and his teeth were together.

"Boy, you got yourself a nasty shiner there, don't ya', chum?" he asked. "Where'd ya' get that nasty thing?"

"Clam it, Ape," I said. "I'm on business. Lemme talk to Febreezi."

The Ape raised his lips slightly in what I could only assume was his attempt at a grin.

"What does it take to teach you a lesson?" he asked.

"A lot less than it would take to teach you how to read," I replied.

"Real funny, Astronaut," he said, eyeballing my trousers. "That's a nice lump in your pocket. No one sees the boss without giving me his piece, first."

"No need to get fresh, Ape," I said, reaching into my pocket and pulling out my pistol. The Ape took the gun and hid it somewhere on his enormous body.

"All right, go ahead, smart guy. But I'm warning you, Astronaut ... I got my eye on you."

"You and everyone else in the world," I said.

Febreezi sat real smug and tight in his desk chair. Precariously balanced atop his royal blue hair, a tall helmet with a sunburst design licking the edges made his head look three feet tall. On his torso, he sported a shimmering dinner jacket, a ruffled sharkstooth shirt, and a furry bowtie, as was the latest style. I couldn't tell what he had on below the waist, but from the looks of his upper half, I could only guess that it was probably twice as queer. He had a phone implanted in his ear, and when he talked into it, he looked like a loon. When I walked in, he motioned at me to sit in front of his desk as he finished his conversation.

"... and 500 cases of the Palisades Chagrine. Yup. Yeah, you know what I want, Tony. Say 'hi' to that beautiful wife of yours."

He hung the phone up, or so I assumed; it was difficult to tell with phone implants. He rose out of his chair halfway so that I could get a glimpse of his bright green plaster trousers. Just as I suspected, exactly twice as queer.

"Say, Astronaut, it sure is nice to see ya'!" he said, throwing his hand out.

I declined to shake it. "I wish I could say the same to you, Febreezi. What's the big deal siccing your henchman on me like that?"

"Oh, gee, I'm sorry about that, Astronaut," he said, settling back into his chair, "I really am. That was a real mix-up, all right. I had it under advisement that you were trying to put an end to my little deal here. Now that I know you're on the up-and-up, well, hey, no problemo!"

No problemo. Febreezi talked so slick you could use his saliva to style your hair. Martha was the only person who knew I had anything to do with the deal; I could only imagine who his "advisor" was.

Febreezi leaned back in his chair and threw his legs up on the desk.

"Getting in an order of some good Chagrine, Astronaut," he said. "You ever drink Chagrine?"

I shook my head.

"Don't much go in for the soft stuff," I said.

"It's a shame," he answered. "You might be pleasantly surprised. Next time, I guess."

"Let's cut to the chase, Febreezi," I said. "Martha came to me and asked me to check into your little business proposition. I was prepared to snoop this thing out, but my head was visited by a little piece of wood that told me I should approach this one differently. So I'm on the level with you; howsabout you get on the level with me? What's this thing all about, anyway?"

A glimmer of excitement danced across Febreezi's purple contacts.

"I appreciate your honesty, Astronaut. What I'm about to tell you is not to leave this room, do you understand?"

"Cut the drama, Febreezi," I said. "You say you've got a business deal; I need some business. I wanna know what you've got up your puffy sleeve."

Febreezi leaned back in his chair and whistled. "You're a tough customer, Astronaut. All right, I'll tell you. Rare books."

"Rare books?" I asked, raising an eyebrow. I didn't expect that.

"Yeah, rare books. I'm a collector. All this," he waved his hands in the air, "all this doesn't mean a thing to me. It's the family business. Rare books, that's where my passion lies, Astronaut."

It made for a nice spiel, all right, but it sounded awful fishy.

"Why would you want to go legit when you're obviously making a killing here?" I asked.

"Because I'm not making a killing. It looks nice, but Central D. takes a huge cut. I get my money vested in legitimate enterprises, and eventually I can come clean."

"No way. Once you're in with Central D., you're in for life. They got a lotta dirt on you, Febreezi, you know that. No way they'll let you go legit."

"I got a lotta dirt on them, too," said Febreezi. "I got a lotta dirt on everybody. I even got dirt on you, Astronuat."

"Dirt can easily be swept up," I said.

"Not when it's ingrained in the carpet," Febreezi countered.

"Well, I'll be sure to bring my vacuum, then," I said.

"Vacuums are a void," Febreezi said, a smile tickling the corners of his mouth. "And a void is filled with nothing."

"So's your head," I replied.

"Touché."

"I hate to leave during this delicious display of wit, Febreezi," I said, pushing my chair back and standing up, "but I got other clients' problems to take care of."

"Say, Astronaut," Febreezi said through a mild smirk, "It sure was nice seeing ya'. Give my best to that beautiful ex-wife of yours. Tell her she's welcome to drop that check off anytime."

"I'll make sure she runs right over," I said.

5

After I left the casino, I stopped by the bank to deposit the money I had earned on Aquari. I knew my habits too well to trust myself with 50 large in cash. All it would take was one more visit to Febreezi and an open afternoon to send my bank account right back into the graveyard.

As I was leaving, the security guard held the door open for me. "Have a good afternoon, Mr. Astronaut," he said.

I paused in the doorway and turned to look at him. He didn't look familiar to me.

"How did you know my name?" I asked him.

He smiled.

"New bank policy," he said. "I know everyone's name."

A little old lady brushed past me and through the door.

"Have a nice afternoon, Mrs. Danvers," he said to her.

"That's not my name," she said over her shoulder.

When I got back to the office, the door was cracked open and Martha's legs were propped up on my coffee table. I walked into the main room and stood in front of her. She gave me a look that could've melted diamonds. I knew that look. It meant she wanted something and she was prepared to use everything in her arsenal to get it. I knew Martha's arsenal well and I didn't trust myself when threatened with it.

"Hi Johnny," she said, exhaling a plume of smoke in my direction. Martha's smoke always lingered a little longer than it should have, but when it went away, you missed it. "Where ya' been?"

"Just been," I said, cool with a cigarette of my own.

She gave me a bewitching smile and moved her legs from the coffee table to the couch. If there was one thing Martha knew, it was the art of seduction. Her powers were strong and evil. Every subtle shift in her body movements, every inflection on every word out of her mouth, they all worked together toward a single common goal. I went over that morning's Clinton Downs stats in my head in an attempt to quell the beast. I didn't remember a horse named "Sex" showing up on the stat sheet, but somehow, there he was, smack dab in the middle of every race.

"So tell me the truth, Johnny," she said. "Were you talking to Febreezi? Or have you been seeing another dame? Are you finally over me," hiking her skirt up and flashing me the bedroom eyes, "... forever?"

I moved over to the other side of the room and sat down in the chair that kept me furthest from temptation. I lit up another Palmetto to calm my nerves. It was seven o'clock and I hadn't indulged in a single sin since the night before. If I could make it a couple more hours, I could break my record.

I could not break my record.

Forty-five minutes later, I was suffering from the complete onslaught of Martha's arsenal back at my apartment. Her torpedoes were particularly punishing this evening. The battle ended with her trapping my seamen in a hollow.

She collapsed on the bed next to me. We were both sweating from the struggle and the January heat.

"So what did you find out?" she asked. This was her style. Cut right to the chase in a moment of weakness. She had been using the same trick for years, and, against my better judgment, it always worked.

"Not much. I don't think he's on the level. I never had Febreezi pegged as a bibliophile."

"What is that?" Martha asked. "What does that have to do with time travel?"

"A bibliophile is someone who loves books," I answered, slightly confused. "As far as I know, that has nothing to do with time travel. But it does have everything to do with the rare book dealership he's starting."

Martha rolled over on her side and propped her head up with an arm. God, those torpedoes were magnificent weapons.

"Listen, genius," Martha said, tersely, "I don't know a thing about any rare book dealership and I don't give a lick. Febreezi wants me to invest in some kinda time travel scheme."

I snorted.

"Time travel scheme?" I scoffed. "That sounds even fishier. As in, non-existent. If you had told me from the start that he wanted you to invest in a time travel scheme, I would've told you to save your money, and I could have saved myself one helluva miserable day."

Martha slumped back onto the bed.

"It's not impossible, you know," she said. "Some of the shuttles go nearly the speed of light already."

"Nearly the speed of light is not the speed of light, Doll," I answered. "It's never gonna happen because the second something hits the speed of light it ceases to exist."

Martha laughed cynically.

"Now who sounds ridiculous?" she said. "Boy, what kind of mumbo-jumbo did they teach you at that detective college, anyway?"

"The mumbo-jumbo that says there's no such thing as time travel," I answered.

Martha arose from the bed and strolled over to the dresser, where she had left her purse. She shuffled through the contents and pulled out a sealed envelope, which she brought back to the bed and handed to me. Through the envelope, I could make out the shape of a check.

"I want you to give this to Guy Febreezi," she said. "Tell him it's a little something to help him get started."

I took the envelope.

"But you don't even know what you're investing in," I said.

"I got a hunch," she answered. "Besides, I like taking chances."

"There is no such thing as chance," I said.

"Spoken like a man who has no luck," she answered.

6

The next morning I woke up early to pay another visit to Guy Febreezi. In every case I've ever taken, there comes a point when satisfying my own curiosity becomes more important than getting paid. I wasn't getting paid for this case, anyway, so curiosity was pretty much all I had to go on.

I left my apartment and headed west on the Vicious Turnpike toward Bontemps. The Vicious ran straight through the middle of Outer Borzoi's six boroughs—Bontemps, Florin, Peaks Park, Brahlia, Oceanside, and The Grove. Each borough was, in turn, divided into several districts. My apartment, for instance, was in the Midpoint District of Florin, while my office was a couple of miles away in the Lantern District of the same borough. Bontemps was the westernmost borough on the other side of the John Henry Bridge.

I took the Pulliver Street exit and drove about two miles down to the casino. I was lucky enough to find a parking spot right at the front of the lot. I parked my car and walked into the factory façade. The Remolian with the laser pistol sat inside, reading a magazine twice his size. He looked up as I walked in and grimaced.

"Nice to see ya' again, Astronaut," he squeaked. "But we ain't hiring."

"Good, 'cause I ain't applying," I said. "Lemme talk to the boss man, Tiny."

The Remolian grumbled as he dialed the extension on his communicator.

"Astronaut's here again," he said, then paused to listen to the voice on the other end. "I don't know, lemme ask."

"You got a check with ya'?" he asked me.

"I got an envelope," I answered. "What's inside is anybody's guess."

The Remolian conveyed this information to Febreezi.

"Right," he said into the communicator, "I'll send him right in."

I walked past him and onto the casino floor.

"Hey, Astronaut," he shouted after me.

I spun around and faced him.

"Can you flip this page for me?"

The Ape stood in his usual position outside of Febreezi's office.

"Back again so soon, Astronaut?" he asked. "You falling in love with the boss?"

"No worries, Ape," I said. "I would never dream of stealing your boyfriend."

The Ape racked his brain for a suitable comeback. I stood in silence, staring at him as he contorted his face into jellyfish shapes.

"He ain't my boyfriend," he finally said.

"Quick thinking, Ape," I replied. "I can only imagine the comebacks that you discarded on the path to that little gem."

He sneered.

"All right, smart guy. You know the rules. Lemme see what yer packin'."

I handed him my pistol.

"I hope you realize I'm biting my tongue right now," I cracked.

"Get in there before ya' get clobbered, wisenheimer," he said.

Where wit fails, the threat of physical violence succeeds. I had to admit, it worked on me. Whoever said the pen is mightier than the sword must've been using an awfully dull sword.

I opened the door to Febreezi's office. As I walked in, I saw him hastily slip something into the top drawer of his desk. The more time you spend doing detective work, the more you learn to read body language and to get a sense of suspicious behavior when it is occurring ... and from where I was standing, Febreezi looked awfully suspicious. Not to mention ridiculous—he had really pulled out all the stops when getting dressed that morning. His screaming pink shirt was topped with an enormous feathered collar that rose a foot above his head like a peacock's tail. On his face, he wore a pair of racing goggles, which I would bet had never seen any racing time.

"Nice outfit, Febreezi," I said. "You taking part in a gay demolition derby later?"

Febreezi chuckled.

"Amazing, Astronaut," he said. "You don't miss a word."

"I'm not exactly sure what that means," I said.

"Good," he answered, mysteriously. "So where's the check?"

"It's hiding in the same place as your manners," I replied, walking over to the bar. "Mind if I pour myself a drink?"

Febreezi flashed a crooked alligator grin.

"Of course, Johnny," he said. "We got in that Chagrine this morning. Have a taste; it's nice and toasty."

I poured myself a gin and tonic instead, then walked over to the chair in front of his desk and sat down. I took a sip of the drink. Not too shabby. Febreezi stocked his bar with nothing but top-shelf stuff. I decided I needed to stop in and visit more often.

Febreezi leaned back in his chair and stared at me. He seemed impatient. Just the way I liked it. Before I gave him his check, I intended to make him sweat a little.

"Seems there's a little confusion about this whole business proposition, Febreezi," I began. "Seems Martha got a slightly different story than I did about where this money is going. As in, completely different. Before I can give you this check, I'm going to have to ask you to level with me."

Febreezi nodded.

"Of course, Johnny," he said in fake earnestness, "anything you need to know."

I raised the glass to my lips and took another sip, cool and collected.

"Whaddya know about time travel?" I asked.

Febreezi nodded again. Serious.

"I know a lot about a lot of things," he said.

"Quit bluffing me, buster," I said. "I know what you told Martha and I know what you told me. Now quit your chewing and spit."

The door suddenly flung open. I swiveled my chair around to see the Ape standing in the doorway.

"Boss," the Ape said, "can I talk to you outside for a minute?"

"I guess I don't really have a choice," Febreezi answered.

"You've always got a choice, Boss," the Ape answered. "It's what makes us human."

"I wouldn't be so sure of that," Febreezi said, his eyes twinkling.

He pushed himself back from his desk and rose from his chair. 'How many pairs of plaster trousers does this guy have?' I wondered. As he stood, he flashed me the plastic choppers.

"Will you excuse me for a moment?" he asked.

"Of course," I said. "I'm about due for another drink, anyway."

Febreezi followed the Ape out of the office and shut the door behind him. I knew I had to act fast. I stood up from my chair and walked around to the other side of the desk. I tugged on the top drawer. Locked. Luckily, I was no slouch when it came to breaking and entering. The locks on these desks were as easy to open as an eighteen-year-old girl on prom night.

I pulled a credit card out of my wallet and slid it across the top of the drawer. With just a little wiggle, the lock snapped free. I opened the drawer.

Lying face down on top of a stack of papers was an old, battered paperback. I grabbed the book and shut the drawer up tight, using the credit card to jimmy the lock back into position.

I slid the book into my inner suit pocket and hot-footed it over to the bar. I would have time to examine the book later. I sloppily filled my glass and returned to my chair like nothing had happened.

Febreezi came back in, flustered and apologetic.

"I'm sorry, Johnny," he said, "but there's a bit of a mess out here that I have to take care of. A word of advice should you ever start a casino: never extend credit to a Ptsaurian."

"That's fine, Febreezi," I said. "I was on my way out, anyway."

I stood up from the chair and walked to the door.

"Say, Johnny," Febreezi said, "aren't ya' forgetting something?"

I reached into my pocket and handed Febreezi the envelope that Martha had given me.

"I realize that you never answered my question," I said.

Febreezi grinned and snatched the envelope out of my hand.

"Pleasure, Johnny," he giggled.

"Aren't you forgetting something, too?" I asked the Ape.

He grunted and handed me my pistol.

"Don't hurt yourself, Astronaut," he said dryly.

"We always hurt the ones we love," I answered.

7

When I got back to my car, Martha was waiting in the passenger seat. I opened the door and climbed in next to her.

"Nice to see you again, Martha," I said. "And by nice I mean miserable."

"Shut up and drive, Johnny," she responded.

I pulled out of the parking lot and onto Pulliver.

"I would be driving if you hadn't said anything, you know," I told her. "That's what I do in my car. I drive."

"Oh, Johnny," she said, turning to me and batting her eyelashes. "Why must we fight like cats and dogs?"

"Because you're a cat and I'm a dog," I said, simply. "What are you doing in my car, Martha?"

"I wanted to stop you, Johnny," she said. "I've got a bad feeling about this business deal. I don't think you should give him the check."

"You're too late, toots," I said. "I just dropped the money off."

Martha looked at me in a panic.

"You have to get it back, Johnny," she said. "I made a mistake. I can't ... we can't go through with this."

I turned onto the Vicious Turnpike and headed east, back toward my apartment.

"What are you talking about, ya' dingbat?" I asked. "First you tell me to give him the check, then you tell me to get it back ... you tell me you're investing in time travel, Febreezi tells me it's a book dealership? I wash my hands of this whole crazy mess. If you wanna get your money back, you go get it back."

Martha pursed her lips, folded her arms, and collapsed back into her seat, letting out a "humph," to let me know she wasn't happy with the situation. Martha was unpleasant enough to be around on a normal basis, but when she didn't get her way—oh you kid. I had long since learned not to be affected by her temper tantrums. Martha was like a small child who'd scraped her knee ... all tears and self-pity until someone gave her a balloon to play with.

"Listen, Martha," I said. "I don't know if this Febreezi thing is on the up-and-up, but you made your bed, and now you have to lie in it."

"Trouble is," she answered, "I'm not the only one who's going to be lying in it."

"Whaddya mean by that?" I asked.

"I had a little meeting with Charvez this morning. He didn't come right out and say anything, but I think Central D. knows what Febreezi is up to. I think they're going to try to put a stop to it, and if they do, our little deal is going to be held up to the light."

"Well, that's what you get for making friends who are paper-thin," I said. "I'd love to be concerned for you, Martha, but it ain't my problem. I'm just the messenger. Whatever you and Febreezi have going is none of my concern."

"You're right, Johnny," she said quietly. "It's my problem. I'll take care of it."

"Damn straight," I answered.

Martha turned to look out the window.

"Johnny?" she asked. "Can I ask you a question?"

"Shoot, dollface," I said.

"If you had it all to do over again, what would you change?"

The first thought that popped into my head was, "I wouldn't have married you." Some things, unfortunately, you just can't say to a dame, no matter how much she's bugging ya'.

"I don't know, Martha," I said, turning off the Vicious Turnpike onto Bacardi Street. "I guess maybe I would've been a little more careful with my finances or something. How 'bout you?"

"I wouldn't have married you," she answered.

Martha invited herself up to my place for a cocktail. This time, I planned on showing her the door before she had a chance to seduce me. This time, I was going to be strong.

This time didn't quite work out the way I planned.

After a nice, spine-shattering workout, we lay in bed together and sweated. I'll admit, as much as Martha upset me, there was something comfortable about sweating with her. I never had to put on an act for Martha. I could be as filthy and rotten as I wanted to be and she couldn't say "boo," 'cause she was twice as filthy and rotten as I could ever be.

Trouble was, I didn't necessarily like being filthy and rotten.

Sure, it was good for kicks every now and again, but it was no way to live your life. Call me an old softie, but I still held out hopes that there was something nice waiting for me out there in the world. I didn't ask for much. A pretty dame to lie down with at night and enough money to play the ponies every once in awhile would be good enough for me. Better, at any rate, than this world of sin and corruption that I was living in now.

I thought about the question Martha asked me earlier. The real answer was, if I could go back in time, I would have changed a lot. For starters, I would have never gotten involved in that whole business back in July.

A guy I knew from detective school had called me up last July and asked me to do some investigative work for him on a job that he was too busy to handle. Business was slow and the money was good, so I took the case. Came to find out later that it had all been a setup. My "friend" from detective school had been working for Central Development. Central D. had been auditing the local P.I.s for their "adherence to community standards," as the subpoena said. They caught me doing a few things that, legally, I shouldn't have been doing, and they slapped an enormous fine on me—the same fine that Martha recently paid off, saving my business from the junk heap. It was then that I met Charvez, and he has been up my butt ever since, like an angry piece of corn that refuses to join its friends in the toilet.

I guess I should've been grateful to Martha for helping me pay off my debts. Without her, I might have had to move on from my world of seedy criminals, philandering wives, and bureaucratic nonsense. Yep, she was a real saint, all right. If I was a fish back in the olden days of evolution, she would've been the one telling me not to leave the water.

"You can't walk, you idiot," she would have said. "Stay down here in the mud with me."

"Burble burble," I would have answered, because I would have been a fish.

8

A few hours and several punishing blows later, Martha took off, and I caught a second wind. It was called the urge to purge myself of her memory. I glanced at my watch—10:30. On a Thursday night, that meant just one thing. It was time for some disco.

I hopped in the car and drove out to the Toilet off of Route D74. The Toilet used to be a Ptsaurian joint until the Petruskans moved in and pushed the Ptsaurians out. Although I was Petruskan by birth, I didn't really feel any strong connection to my roots. Not like some of the cheeseballs who frequented the Toilet, with their slicked back hair and their curlicue moustaches. For all the limitations of the crowd, though, the Toilet was the only disco worth its salt in the city. I could get drunk in any fleabag hole-in-the-wall in Borzoi, but when I needed to dance, I needed a joint that jumped.

I parked in my usual spot behind the club, got out of the car, and made my way to the front of the velvet rope. I was wearing the brand new silver suit I picked up on Aquari and I was feeling hot; I mean *sparkplug*. I strode up the front steps with a shuffle in my step and the knowledge that I would, without a doubt, be the wildest looking space P.I. in the house that evening.

"Hey, Johnny Astronaut, spectacular suit, baby."

Rascal, the doorman, knew me as well as you know any guy you talk to for two minutes a week. Sometimes three if I was finishing a smoke. I nodded to him—cool as a block of dry ice—and walked past him into the club.

I walked briskly down the carpeted stairs and over to the bar. A lady was sitting in my seat. I briefly considered doing the chivalrous thing and letting her remain where she was. Then I got a whiff of the chocolaty scent of her Ruskan perfume and came to my senses. You didn't treat Ruskans gentle where I was from, lady or not.

I tapped her on the shoulder.

"Hey Ruskan," I said. "You're in my seat."

She turned around and glared at me, fire in her eyes. Truth be told, I could give a rat's backward tail about our racial differences. Like I said, I was hardly waving the Petruskan flag around. But in a Petruskan bar, we got first dibs, and I wasn't about to fight any system that worked to my advantage, especially since so few actually did.

She stood up and walked to the other end of the bar, but not without spitting out a sarcastic, "Yes, sir." I settled into my seat. It was good to be back home.

"Hey, Astronaut, whattaya' have?"

I glanced up into the bartender's face and felt a twinge of recognition. This wasn't the normal bartender, Boris, but there was something familiar about him. I had seen this guy somewhere before.

"Where's Boris?" I asked.

"Boris hasn't been around for awhile," he said. "Name's Henry. I'm the new bartender."

I nodded.

"I'm Johnny Astronaut."

Henry smiled. "I know."

Of course he did. I was a legend.

"You look familiar to me, Henry. Do I know you from somewhere?" I asked.

"Yep," he said. "I'm a security guard at your bank during the day. I saw you in there yesterday."

That was it.

"Well, Henry," I said, laying my bankcard down on the counter, "your bank is about to make me a very happy man. I'll take an Old-Fashioned, if you'd please."

"Right away, boss," he winked.

As I waited for my drinks, I thought about the Febreezi situation. Martha's unexpected appearance made me completely forget about the book I had stolen. I was considering making the hike back to my apartment to pick it up, when I became aware of a cool sensation trickling down the back of my neck. I jerked my head up and the floodgates opened. Water ran down my head, soaking the top of my new suit. The Ruskan chick stood next to my chair, holding an empty, overturned glass in her mitts. I rose up from my chair and planted an open-handed slap across her face. She stared at me with defiance in her eyes.

"If you lay your hand on me again, I'll kill you," she said.

Something about her courage gave me pause. If any of the Petruskans out on the dance floor had been able to hear what was happening, the girl would have been run out of the club on a rail. I happened to have a soft spot for an underdog, especially when the underdog had a tail that could wag an elephant.

"Listen," I said, "I'm gonna let you go this time. Next time you might not be so lucky."

"Tough talk," she answered. "But from where I'm standing, you're all wet."

"I've been wetter," I said. "Now get lost or I might make you wet, too."

The girl remained. I tried to play casual, but her attitude was giving me the shivers in a good way. She stared me down with eyes that could have lit dynamite.

"You're Johnny Astronaut," she said.

"So they tell me," I responded.

"They say you're the best."

"They don't lie."

"You don't look that great to me."

"Try me."

"Permission to dance."

"Permission granted."

Henry returned from wherever he was returning from with my drink and my bankcard.

"Here ya' go, Johnny," he said. "Old-Fashioned, nice and stiff. One thing, though ... the bankcard didn't go through. It says you have no money in your account."

"That's funny," I said. "I just made a big deposit yesterday. You saw me."

"That I did," he agreed. "The deposit must not have gone through yet. That's okay, Johnny. Your money's no good here."

"Thanks, chum," I answered, raising the glass in a salute.

"Have a good dance, Johnny," he answered.

"Always do," I said.

I downed the drink in one gulp and followed the girl out to the middle of the dance floor. The opening strains of Chic's "Le Freak" bounded out of the speakers. As we stepped onto the crowded floor, the patrons cleared a path for us. I might not have been a rich man, a handsome man, or an honest man, but I owned this floor and everyone in that place knew it.

I placed my right arm around the girl's waist and my left hand on her shoulder. She stared into my eyes. On the count of three, we launched into an American Hustle. Her right foot went out in perfect sync with my left. I closed my eyes and felt the music sweep over me.

I spun her out and back into my body, turning her around into a perfect Foxy Trot. This girl seemed to have the moves, all right, but I had to see how she did without my lead. I spun her back out to my side and let go of her hands. In perfect time, we both launched into a Bus Stop. Her arms flung out passionately, her body consumed by the dance. Our racial differences melted away as we jived in perfect symmetry.

I was suddenly overtaken by the age-old desire to do a little showboating. The greatest thing about disco, in my opinion, was its connection to the roots of human nature. When I heard that wah-wah bass jumping over the 2-4 beat, I became ancient man, virility coursing out of my pores and into the noses of every sweet little biddy in the joint.

I stepped into the middle of the floor. By this time, everyone else in the club had stopped to watch the mating ritual unfold. The girl knew what to do ... she did the Walk in place as I leapt into my signature move, the Triple Step, followed by a perfectly executed Russian Walk which ended in a knee-slide right on the downbeat. A cheer arose from the crowd; this was what they came to see.

As I slid across the floor, the girl did a standing flip over my head. We were on fire now. I somersaulted into the splits and back up to catch her right at the beginning of a Latin Twist which culminated in a flawless Latin Hustle with the extra sidestep thrown in for kicks. The music swelled, and we parted ways for the big finale.

I boogied in place as she reared up at the end of the catwalk for the final lift. She ran toward me. I kept my hands at my side ... raise them a split second too early and suddenly you're doing a "move." The trick was to make it look spontaneous.

Her feet barely touched the ground as she bounced down the catwalk toward me. The crowd gasped ... can they do it? I remained cool as a frozen lab cat, feeling the music in every cell of my being. I knew when she was going to jump. I was prepared.

We couldn't have choreographed it better. Right at the beginning of the final bar, she jumped. My arms went up to grab her around the waist in midair. We spun and spun as the bar came to a close, ultimately ending precisely on the final beat in a freeze that could have been bronzed and put into a museum. The crowd erupted in wild applause. My chest heaved and my pants ached.

She slid down my body and came to rest on the floor, staring into my eyes.

"Let's get out of here," she said. "Now."

9

I opened my eyes. Sunlight screamed in through my window and punched me in the face like a branding iron. I closed my eyes again. It was no use. The sunlight breached my defenses in a full-frontal attack. It was a formidable adversary and I knew when I was defeated.

I raised myself up on my arms and looked around the room. My bedroom looked like it had spent the night caught in a tornado. My silver suit dangled from the ceiling fan. The goldfish bowl that had not housed goldfish for several months now did not even house water—all of the liquid inside had relocated to my area rug where it had more room to spread out. My underwear was nowhere to be seen, but I could say for certain that it was no longer covering my body.

The previous night's events existed only in flashes. As far as I could remember, there had been some sort of a car ride back to my apartment, followed by some sort of a drinking session, followed by some sort of intense black void. My sheets and comforter looked as though they had been run through a paper shredder and then glued back together. For all I knew, they had been.

I rubbed the crust out of my eyes and painfully swung my legs onto the floor. I suddenly became aware that my bladder was on the verge of committing suicide. I ran into the bathroom and unleashed the previous night's alcohol in a satisfying flood. As the final drops joined their comrades-in-bowl, I glanced over at the mirror. Written on the glass in red lipstick was a note.

It said, "We will meet again."

Just then, the phone rang.

I walked out of the bathroom and picked up the receiver.

"Hello?" I answered.

"Johnny?"

It was Martha. She sounded like she was crying. Maybe she had come to the realization that she was a terrible person and she was crying over all of the pain she had caused me and everyone else who knew her over the course of her life. Or maybe she had stepped on a tack. Either way, I would have been satisfied.

"Johnny," she sobbed. "Johnny, you have to come over to my house right away."

"Thanks for the invite, Martha," I replied, "but I was planning on brushing my teeth and then staring at the wall for the next ten hours."

I spied my other suit coat from the previous day draped over the back of my living room chair, and I was suddenly reminded of Febreezi's book. I held the phone with my shoulder and checked the inside pocket. The book was gone.

"Johnny," she wailed, "listen to me. You have to come over here right away."

"Yeah, I heard you the first time," I said. "What's the big rush?"

"Guy Febreezi is dead."

She gave a final wail and the line went dead.

I set the receiver back on the cradle. Unfortunately, I knew Martha a little too well, and I knew that she didn't cry unless she was up to something. If Guy Febreezi was really dead, Outer Borzoi was about to see some serious consequences. I would have turned on my telescreen and checked the news if it hadn't been reduced to a gaping hole by a certain ape-like friend of mine.

I walked up the front stairs of my old house and rang the doorbell. The yard looked pretty good. I wondered how many gardeners Martha had to boff to keep it that way. Nice how life has its way with you; you work hard, save up, get yourself a nice place, and then your wife takes most of it away and your lawyer takes the rest. I reminded myself to never fall in love again. Or if I did, I should at least check her papers before the wedding and make sure she was human.

Martha came to the door looking like hell had given her a day pass. She stuck her head out and scanned the street nervously.

"Were you followed?" she asked.

"The only thing following me is the dark cloud of despair," I answered. "From the looks of things, he's caught onto your trail, too."

I stepped into the house. Martha locked the three deadbolts and stretched the safety chain across the jamb. I didn't remember the place being such a fortress when I was living there. Of course, when I was living there, the fear of death at the hands of a spurned lover was not quite so omnipresent.

Even though it was the middle of the day, the curtains were closed and the house was shrouded in darkness.

"I like what you've done with the place, Martha," I said. "I hear the dank cavern look is quite in vogue this year."

Martha looked at me and burst into tears.

"Oh, Johnny!" she wailed, throwing her arms around me. "It was horrible!"

"There, there," I said, glancing at my watch behind her back. "Everything's going to be all right."

"Murdered!" she gasped. "Blood everywhere! Gore! It was horrible!"

"Now listen, Martha," I said, putting my hands on her shoulders and pushing her away from me. "You've got to pull yourself together. For Guy."

Martha sniffled. Her bottom lip quivered. She was a shoe-in for best actress.

I walked away from her and over to the bar. Looked like the only thing of mine that she didn't sell was the scotch. I poured two glasses for myself and settled down on the couch.

Martha collapsed in the chair next to me and grabbed one of my drinks. She took a long drag on her cigarette and flashed me her best look of distress.

"I went over to Febreezi's office this morning, before the casino opened," she said. "He called me last night and asked me to come over. Said he had some important new information regarding his business proposition. When I arrived, no one was there, not even his gorilla bodyguard. The door to his office had been ripped off its hinges. The place was in complete disarray, Johnny."

"Hell of a thing," I replied, dry as a microwaved cracker.

"You don't know the half of it, Johnny," she said through a stuffy nose. "The gore. The guts and blood. Johnny, it was like a wild animal had torn him apart. Pieces ... scattered everywhere!"

"I hope they destroyed his queer plaster pants while they were at it," I offered.

Martha stared me down with icicle eyes.

"Johnny Astronaut," she said, coldly, "there is nothing amusing about this. I have just been through a horrible, horrible experience. I am turning to you for comfort. I don't know if you quite grasp the magnitude of this situation."

I sighed. "All right. Assuming that Febreezi is really dead, it's going to be big news."

Martha nodded. "It's already big news, Johnny."

Martha flipped on the telescreen. A reporter stood in front of the casino. Across the bottom of the screen was a graphic and headline reading "Gangland Murder."

"... If you're just joining us," the reporter said, "we are coming to you live from the Febreezi factory in Bontemps, where this morning, gangster Guy Febreezi was found brutally murdered."

I stared at the screen in shocked silence.

"Do you see, Johnny?" Martha asked. "I'm not lying to you."

I looked closely at the screen. The reporter was standing across the street from the factory. Police were milling around the front door, sipping coffee and trying to look busy. Directly in front of the factory, two shapes faced one another, locked in what appeared to be intense conversation.

"Martha," I said. "Blow up the background 200%."

She fumbled with the remote.

"I don't know how to work this damn thing," she said, handing the remote to me.

I pressed the correct key combination and zoomed into the background. Standing next to the front door of the factory was Charvez. He was talking to the Ape. The picture was too pixilated to read their lips, but whatever they were saying, it looked intense. Charvez whipped out a phone and dialed a number.

In my pocket, my phone started vibrating.

I pulled my phone out of my pocket and looked at the number. Just as I suspected—Charvez. I picked it up.

"Say, Charvez," I said. "I was just watching you on the telescreen. You're looking good. Will you wave to me?"

On the telescreen, Charvez stuck up a blurry middle finger.

"Meet me at the station in fifteen minutes," he said. "I've got some questions for you about our unfortunate friend here."

"Unfortunate friend?" I asked. "If you're talking about the Ape standing next to you, all I can say is that I'm sorry he's so ugly."

"Fifteen minutes, Astronaut," Charvez barked before he hung up. "The clock is ticking."

With the promise that I would return after my meeting with Charvez and the knowledge that I would do nothing of the sort, I left Martha holed up in her fortress and took the Vicious Turnpike out to Central Development in the Basha district.

10

I opened the door to Charvez's office as far as it could go, which wasn't very far. Official-looking documents snagged on the bottom of the door as I swept it open, crunching into malformations and tearing apart. I glanced down at one that appeared to be an undelivered stay of execution. It was dated over two weeks prior.

I had never been inside Charvez's office before. I can't say I was impressed. I always figured Charvez whiled away his hours in some kind of dank little pit with unfinished paperwork stacked everywhere. In actuality, Charvez whiled away his hours in some kind of dank little pit with unfinished paperwork haphazardly tossed everywhere.

Charvez looked up as I struggled with the door.

"Yer late," he said, sternly.

"I would've been on time, but it's a madhouse out there," I replied. "I had to fight my way through a crowd of reporters to get to the front desk."

Charvez stared me down in what I could only guess was an

earnest attempt at intimidation. It fit him about as well as his cheap suit.

I tripped my way through the paper snow and sat down in the chair in front of his desk.

"Did I invite you to take a seat?" he asked.

"Sorry," I answered. "It just feels so homey in here, I couldn't help but relax."

Charvez kept up the cold stare. I returned a stare that was even colder. Icicles shot out of our eyes and collided in midair, where they broke into fragments that disappeared in the mess of papers covering Charvez's desk. Finally, he spoke.

"How's Martha?" Charvez asked.

"Wouldn't know," I said, nonchalantly. "Haven't seen her."

Charvez opened his mouth in a wry smile.

"I'm sure you haven't," he said. "I'm sure you didn't come here directly from her place."

I smiled back and nodded. Charvez had nothing on me. It wasn't his style to hold anything back. He took a guess and hit the jackpot; too bad he'd never collect the winnings.

"Listen, Johnny," he continued, "we've got you over a barrel here and you know it. If you're hiding something, now is the time to come clean."

"You could stand to do a little cleaning yourself, Charvez," I said. "Now that you're a telly star, maybe you should think about taking a shower."

Charvez slumped against the back of his chair.

"Yer a real pill, Astronaut," he said, "a real pill. Jokes, jokes, jokes, that's all I ever get outta you."

Charvez suddenly bolted forward in his seat and pointed a

shaky finger in my face.

"Enough with the small talk, Astronaut," he said. "What's yer alibi?"

I yawned.

"Don't have one."

Charvez smiled.

"Yer gonna need one, bub."

He reached into his pocket, pulled out a piece of paper and handed it to me. It was a canceled check. More specifically, it was one of my checks. Made out in the amount of 50,000 cubits to Guy Febreezi.

I silently cursed Martha and tossed the check down on Charvez's desk.

"This isn't my handwriting," I said.

"It's your check," Charvez answered.

If I had any faith that Charvez was interested in justice, I would have turned over Martha in a heartbeat. But I knew what he wanted. He could have cared less who murdered Guy Febreezi. He just wanted his cut.

"Here's what we know," Charvez began, "I had a little talk with Martha yesterday, and we know that she's been awful chummy with Guy Febreezi as of late. We know that yer wife went to considerable lengths to get yer debts squared away, and we know that you have been under her employment since then. We also know that Guy Febreezi has been in quite a bit of financial difficulty lately, and that he's been poking his nose around, trying to find some new scheme. Now, we find a check, written by you, to Guy Febreezi, on the same day that Mr. Febreezi is mysteriously murdered. It doesn't take a hyperplane captain to know that the events are related."

The pieces of the puzzle suddenly became fuzzy. I wasn't aware that Febreezi was in any sort of financial difficulty. Maybe I wasn't cut out for this detective business. I would have to think fast to get out of this one.

"All right, Charvez," I said. "I'll tell you what you want to know."

Charvez leaned forward and wet his lips, a wolf on the chicken hunt.

"Febreezi was trying to get into the book business. Seems he wasn't too happy with the muscle you guys were applying. Seems he was looking to go legit. Now, I don't know how that check ended up in his office, but I do know that a certain ugly Ape we both know and love broke into my apartment the other day and smashed my telescreen in two. If I were you, I'd haul him in here and have him explain the whole situation to you."

"Never mind the check, Astronaut," Charvez said. "Let's talk about this book business. Did Febreezi happen to mention any of his titles?"

"I couldn't tell you any names," I answered, "but I know that they had something to do with time travel."

A twisted smile broke out at the edge of Charvez's word hole. He stared into my eyes, trying to see if there was anything more that I was hiding. I had played enough poker in my time to know when to bluff. Charvez may have had the money, and he may have been holding the cards, but he didn't have the face. He might as well have been reading Braille. I gave him nothing.

The buzzing of an intercom interrupted our deadlock. Charvez grimaced and pressed the button on his phone.

"Detective Charvez?" a voice said. "The people from *Nighttime Borzoi* are here to see you."

Charvez either grimaced again, held onto the previous grimace, or fixed his face back into its normal state of grimace. No matter, I had won the battle. Now I had to prepare myself for the war.

"I'll be right out," he answered, then hung up the intercom.

"All right, Astronaut," he said, "I'm gonna let you go. But I'm warning you ... don't go too far. We're keeping our eyes open."

I stood up and smiled.

"It's been a pleasure, Charvez," I said. "We must do this again sometime."

I walked down the station steps towards my car. I was a little distracted by the whirlpool of questions circling through my brain. Why was Martha writing checks from my account? Why was Charvez so interested in knowing what titles Febreezi was planning to sell? What about the book I had stolen? And what did it all have to do with time travel?

I was so distracted, in fact, that I barely noticed the Ruskan woman from the night before getting into a cab right in front of the station.

11

I jumped into my car and floored it out of the parking spot. I caught a glimpse of her cab in the distance. With some careful maneuvering, I managed to get close enough to her to follow.

We drove through the streets of the Basha district at a normal clip. The art of following a car in busy downtown traffic was not unknown to me. Any cabbie worth his weight in hubcaps was used to being followed, so the crafty P.I. had to learn a few tricks to stay incognito. Hang back at the lights, fake turns at the intersections, and always make sure to drive the most popular brand in the most popular color. A good P.I. spent a lot of time in his car and an unobtrusive ride was worth its weight in fake moustaches. I drove a Barclay Vesta. It was a small, inexpensive car, good for parking in tight spots and getting out of tight jams.

The cab pulled up in front of the Good Times bookstore on Continental and Third, well known throughout Outer Borzoi for its fine selection of science fiction and pornography. I managed to find a parking spot close enough to watch the Ruskan as she got out of the cab. She was clutching a book in her hands. I had a pretty good idea which book she clutched.

Seconds after she entered the bookstore, I turned off the engine and got out of my car. I cautiously walked up the sidewalk and into the store.

I kept my head low as I entered. I raised no red flags. Workers at the Good Times were used to customers who sought anonymity.

I ducked into the first aisle and scanned the store from behind a pile of books. She wasn't in immediate view. It was times like this that I regretted my profession. Say a normal person has a night of passionate love and the woman leaves a cryptic message on the mirror, then disappears ... if he sees the girl again, he counters her and asks her to explain herself. I am not a normal person. I am a P.I., and if there's one thing a P.I. learns, it is this: people are not to be trusted. Everyone has an ulterior motive. If a woman screws you and disappears, leaving a cryptic message on your mirror in lipstick, it means that she is a part of something much, much bigger. In some circles, one might say that I was paranoid. In other circles, I was playing it safe. In my circle, and in the circle of questions that was still bouncing around my brain, I had no other choice but to keep my head down and hope to catch the web untangling itself.

I grabbed a book from the shelf nearest me to hide my face, if necessity arose. I cautiously stepped into the next aisle. The Good Times was a labyrinth of book aisles and book stacks and book tables and book displays in an enormous empty room that, through years of collection, was quite the opposite of empty. I did not have a perfect method for tailing someone in a place like the Good Times. One had to carefully balance the fear of getting caught with the reality of being in a place with a lot of nooks and crannies to be searched. The one thing that I had working for me was the element of surprise. She did not know she was being followed.

The desire to see a curiosity fulfilled does strange things to a man. In this case, it made me drop my natural cautious tendencies and start working the room like a sloppy prostitute. I ignored my tailing impulses and brazenly worked my way through the aisles, bold-facedly staring the customers down in a furtive attempt to get to the bottom of a story that didn't exist on the written page.

In the middle of the pornography section, I suddenly ran smack dab into Henry, the bartender/security guard. He was perusing the jack-off books with the look of a real connoisseur. I turned quickly, but it was too late. He saw me.

"Hey, Johnny Astronaut!" he exclaimed loudly.

I turned back around and offered a sheepish smile.

"Hello, Henry," I said, "how's tricks?

"Just looking for some porno," he answered. "Can you believe the selection in this place? Outstanding! Personally, I'm a big fan of the hardcore, deep penetration stuff ..."

The customers around us shot dirty looks in our direction, as could be expected. When a man wants to look at filthy anal magazines, a man likes to do so in peace and quiet.

"... I remember this one time, I saw a video of these four Kilgorian chicks getting gangbanged by a bunch of chicken men ..."

"Listen, Henry," I interrupted, "I hate to be rude, but I'm kind of in the middle of something here."

He grinned.

"I hear ya', Johnny," he said, winking. "Do yourself a favor and take a look at the Ptsaurian fetish mags in aisle twelve. Dirty, dirty stuff."

"I'll make a note of it," I said.

I left Henry and made my way to the science fiction aisles at the back of the store, keeping one eye toward the door, in case she had snuck around behind me and circled back to the checkout while I was temporarily detained.

At the back of the store, in the very last aisle of the very last section, I finally caught a glimpse of her. A shiver of excitement ran up my spine. This was what it was all about, being a private investigator, the moment of "Aha! I caught you!"

I didn't say this, of course. I was a professional, and I had no one to say this to. I made my way to the opposite end of the adjoining aisle so that I could keep an eye on her peripherally.

Out of the corner of my eye, I saw her scanning a row of books. She had no idea I was watching her, or if she did, she certainly didn't let on. Now that I was seeing her in the light, she was even more beautiful than I remembered. My heart began to sweat as I gazed upon her lovely figure, which was decidedly out of place in a section filled with nerds and the books that loved them. Her short dark hair framed a childlike face that appeared younger than her deep eyes would have me believe it was. She strained up to reach a book on a high shelf, and her shirt rose up ever so slightly to reveal the outline of her smooth, lovely belly. I could have stood there and stared at her all day.

In the pocket of my suit coat, I felt my phone vibrating against my body. I pulled the phone out and looked down at the display to see who was calling.

The call was coming from my office.

I didn't answer it. A call from my own office could only mean trouble.

When I looked back up at the aisle facing me, the girl was gone.

12

A couple of things seemed a little out of place when I arrived back at my office. For starters, the lights were on. If there was one thing I didn't tolerate, it was wasted electricity. If there were two things I didn't tolerate, it was people who smashed the glass on my office door to break in. Which, coincidentally, was the other thing that seemed off when I arrived back at my office.

I walked in cautiously, with a cigarette dangling off of my lower lip for effect. The place was in complete disarray. My filing cabinet had been knocked over and my carefully filed files were strewn around the floor like cat carcasses at a Ruskan deli. Save for the door, nothing appeared to be so broken that it couldn't easily be fixed. Except for, maybe, the giant ape who was propped on the floor against the back wall, sobbing.

I stood awkwardly just beyond the doorframe, the cigarette ash dangling limp like a sexual metaphor. The Ape seemed to take no notice of me. Every so often he'd slap his meaty hands against his forehead and make a low guttural moan that seemed to suggest unhappiness. After the third or fourth moan, I could not take it any longer.

"You have a funny way of paying a visit," I said. "I got some windows in the back that are still intact. Maybe if you smashed 'em you'd feel better."

He stared up at me, tears streaming down his face.

"Why'd they do it, Astronaut?" he sobbed. "Why'd they have to kill him?"

I took off my coat and hung it on the bottom of the upside-down coatrack. The cigarette ash fluttered off on a search for clean spots to dirty. I took a couple of paces over to the couch and slumped down on the backwards front of the couch behind the sideways coffee table. The ape may have made a mess of the place, but at least he was thorough.

"I don't know, Ape," I sighed. "But I do know that tearing my office apart won't bring him back."

The ape sucked up a snotty tear and nodded his head.

"I'm sorry, Astronaut, honest I am," he sniffed. "But when I got to your office and ya' weren't here, I didn't know what to do. And then I tried calling you, and ya' didn't answer your phone, and I thought for sure that Central D. had made mincemeat outta ya'."

I lit up another cigarette and inhaled the good, cleansing smoke.

"Why would you care, Ape?" I asked. "I wouldn't exactly say we're best pals."

The Ape shook his head.

"Oh, that was just business, Astronaut. I really think you're a nice person, honest I do. And besides," he said, pulling a note out of his pocket and handing it to me, "Mr. Febreezi left me this note before he was killed."

I unfolded the crumpled piece of notebook paper and read the inside. Written on it in neat penmanship were the words "Protect Johnny Astronaut."

"He musta really been looking out for ya'," the Ape said. "He even underlined your name so as I wouldn't get confused."

I flashed him a grim smile and handed the note back to him.

"Ya' gotta help me, Astronaut," he begged. "Ya' gotta track down the bastards what done this. Mr. Febreezi ... he was like a father to me. He always treated me real nice. He bought me popsicles. The kind with three flavors: red, white, and blue. When I walked into the office this morning and seen him like that ..."

The Ape burst into tears. He smashed the back of his fat head against the wall, causing little pieces of plaster to fall from the ceiling.

"Easy, easy!" I shouted. "Jeez, Ape, you're gonna make the whole place fall down!"

The Ape stopped his head bashing and turned his puffy red eyes to me. He looked so miserable and so pathetic that I couldn't help but feel a little sorry for him, even though he was single-handedly responsible for about 1,500 cubits worth of damage to my office and apartment.

"Ah, what the hell," I said. "I gotta get to the bottom of this thing, anyway. Might as well get paid for it."

The Ape slowly grunted his gigantic frame up off the floor. He heaved and wheezed and finally, when he was up on his feet, he held out his paw for a shaking.

I stood up and shook his hand.

"This could be the beginning of a beautiful friendship," I said.

"Fart," he farted.

13

"It is a beautiful day at Clinton Downs. In fact, every day is a beautiful day at Clinton Downs, thanks to Watercress, the makers of the finest environmental rehabilitation systems in the universe. Trust Watercress, because only they can change your world.

"The horses are all lined up and ready to go. There's the pistol ... and they're off!"

I woke up early that morning with the itch. The Ape had put down seven large on his little inquiry, giving me enough pocket change to have a nice little session at the track. It would've been nicer if Martha hadn't stolen my 50,000. Since last night, I had placed several calls to her, to no avail. I didn't want to drive out to her house; it was too risky. Charvez was looking for a chance to nail me, and I was sure he had his eyes all over Casa del Vanderpool right about now. If I was lucky, she'd already skipped town. All in all, 50,000 cubits was a fair price to get rid of Martha for good.

I hadn't placed any bets yet. I was waiting for the third race. Lately, I've been keeping my eye on a horse known as Tindersticks.

He has been in a bit of a slump recently, but I knew his stats from before he transferred to Clinton, and they were real pretty. He was a long shot in a race that I knew he could win, and those odds were sweet. If I put down five grand and hit the jackpot, I would walk the hell out of that racetrack and never look back. I could get away from this place with its murder and corruption, fly off to Desadore and live in a tropical paradise, free from Charvez and Martha and Ape and the whole stinking private investigator life. Yeah, that would be sweet.

I sucked down the last of my Old-Fashioned and made my way to the ticket booths to put my money down. The lines were long today. I fit in well with the dirtbags and alcoholics who frequented Clinton Downs. I hadn't gotten much sleep the night before. This whole mess with Guy Febreezi had me looking over my shoulder at every turn. Every eye felt like it was upon me. Martha had me wrapped up tighter in this affair than a hamster in a pervert's sock. I always knew that she'd be the death of me someday. I just didn't think it was going to be so soon.

In the line next to me, a group of five Ruskans mumbled over the racing program. I got an uneasy feeling from them. I couldn't hear what they were saying, but I felt like they were talking about me. I might have just been paranoid, but I could have sworn one of them jumped out of line and tackled me.

Nope, it wasn't paranoia. I was definitely on the ground with a crazy Ruskan bastard pummeling the living hell out of me. Just what I needed right now—racial trouble. I struggled to throw him off. From somewhere above us, I heard one of his buddies say, "No! We can't hurt him!" The Ruskan eased up and I took my shot, driving my elbow directly into his chest. He let out a gasp and tumbled off of me. I quickly leapt to my feet and took off for the nearest exit.

The Ruskans gave chase. I could hear their heavy work boots clomping against the cement behind me. The exit turnstiles were about 50 feet away. A security guard suddenly appeared in front of the turnstile, blowing his whistle and holding his club in front of him. I faked to the left. He took the bait. He leapt into the air. Spry like a cat, I swerved to the right and he crashed onto the pavement. I ran through the turnstile at full clip and shot out into the parking lot.

I glanced over my shoulder. No one was behind me. Security must have nabbed the Ruskans. Whatever happened, I wasn't going to stick around to find out. I jogged out to my car and headed back to the only place that seemed kind of safe. Kind of.

As soon as I arrived back at my apartment, I flipped the radio on to hear the end of the race. Tindersticks came in first at 60-to-1 odds. Figured.

The phone rang. I answered it. It was what I did when the phone rang.

"Johnny Astronaut," came a woman's voice on the other end of the line.

"Speaking," I said.

"Do you know who this is?"

I hated that.

"I don't know," I answered wearily. "Karen Jamey."

"No," the voice responded. "I said we will meet again, and I meant it. We will meet tonight. Eight o'clock. Calcutta's by the airport. I have your book."

"Wait," I said, before she hung up. "What's your name?"

"Nyla," she answered. "I will see you tonight."

"Good-bye, Nyla," I said.

14

I pulled up to Calcutta's with all the nervous energy of a wound-up gyroscope waiting to unfurl. The girl, Nyla, was an important piece to the puzzle; that much I knew. It was no accident that she happened to steal the book from me. Indeed, our entire meeting, in retrospect, was not accidental. And I was about to find out why.

I walked into the bar and scanned the tables for her face. Scanning tables at Calcutta's was a risky business. Stare too long at a particular patron and you were liable to find yourself without a face. Years spent hanging out with lowlifes had taught me to be discrete about my investigations. I did a quiet sweep of the tables on my way back to an unlit corner. She was nowhere to be seen.

The waitress knew me, but she pretended not to.

"Old-Fashioned," I ordered. Same thing I always ordered from the same waitress. She returned with the same watered-down version at the same wrong price. I gave her more than I owed and got back the same amount of incorrect change.

I sipped my drink and thought about my next move. The one

nice thing about being an investigator was that you often had a privileged view of the bigger picture. These were the facts: Febreezi told Martha that he was working on time travel. He told me that he was dealing in old books. Presumably, from Charvez's reaction, both were true. Nyla stole the book from me that I stole from Febreezi. Martha wrote a check in my name and had me deliver it to Febreezi. Febreezi was now dead. For whatever reason, Febreezi now wanted Ape to protect me.

But what about the Ruskans who had chased me at the track? How did they fit in? And why did Martha get me wrapped up in this whole business to begin with? She obviously didn't need my money if she had enough to pay off my fines with Central D.

I had a feeling that the book was the key. Soon, I would know for sure. Whether my life would ever be the same again was for the gods to determine, if there were any, and if they cared.

Just as I was starting to ache for another Old-Fashioned, Nyla appeared. She was wearing dark sunglasses and a velvet cloak that made her look like she had something to hide. I would have to teach her some tricks if she planned on remaining incognito. The best place to hide, I knew, was in plain sight, and anyone who appeared to be hiding something probably wouldn't be able to keep it hidden for very long.

In this case, her ignorance could very well work to my advantage.

She settled into the booth opposite me and lit up a cigarette. I lit one up as well. We sat in silence, blowing smoke at one another in anticipation of the time when we would begin blowing smoke at one another.

I blew first.

"Where is it?" I asked.

She tapped her cigarette on the side of the ashtray, which sat in the dead center of the table.

"It is safe," she answered, in her mysterious Ruskan drawl.

"You're not," I replied.

"Neither are you," she countered.

I casually let a thin sheet of smoke escape my nostrils. She had her elbow perched on the table, taking drags from her cigarette as though she knew better.

"Would you mind taking off your sunglasses?" I asked.

Her lip twitched slightly. Slowly, she let the weight of the cigarette lower her arm to the ashtray. The cigarette found a nice cozy place to burn and wiggled out of her grasp. She lifted her hand to her face and took the sunglasses off, blinking in the darkness.

It was the first time I had seen them up close since the night we met, and they were stunning. For some reason, blue eyes have always been considered superior to the other colors in terms of attractiveness. Not to me. In my mind, a pair of deep brown betties wins out every time. Nyla's eyes burned with a passion and intelligence far beyond Martha's, or any of the other nameless dames I'd wasted my time on throughout the years. I almost wished she had kept the sunglasses on. Looking into those two little genetic miracles (not to mention the other two genetic miracles located significantly lower than the eyes), I was at a disadvantage.

Somehow, as I tried to catch my breath, the cigarette managed to work its way back between her fingers.

"You have heard about Guy Febreezi, have you not?" she asked me.

I nodded. "What do you know about Febreezi?" I asked.

"Nothing," she said. "I know who killed him and why. That's it."

I tried to read her face and see if she was bluffing. Reading her face was difficult without looking into her eyes, which put me in a strange position as an investigator—if I looked in those eyes, I would lose my impartiality, yet if I didn't look, I couldn't get a good read on her intentions. I had to rely on other signals like the crinkle of the brow and the parting of the lips. She felt honest, but so did my throbbing member, and that lied to me all the time.

"Listen to me, Johnny Astronaut," she said, slowly. "You are in great danger. There are people in this world who think you know more than you do. These people killed Guy Febreezi, and they will kill you as well ... as soon as they learn that you know nothing."

"And when do they learn this?" I asked.

"Guy Febreezi was on to something. Something huge," she continued, ignoring my question. "Against your will, you are a part of it. It is my job to make sure that you get out safely. You must trust me, and you must do as I say, or the entire universe is in peril. Do I make myself clear?"

I scanned her face for emotion. It was like trying to find an ant on the moon with a pair of binoculars.

"Just tell me who did it," I said. "Tell me who did it, and I'll do anything you ask."

"I can't tell you," she said.

"Tell me," I pleaded. "You must tell me."

"I can't tell you, yet," she replied. "Something has to happen first."

The waitress came over and handed me another Old-Fashioned. She asked Nyla what she wanted to drink. Nyla requested a Gimlet.

As the waitress walked away, Nyla leaned over to me.

"What if I told you that everything was predestined? That everything happens for a reason? That somewhere, there is a blueprint for your life, and that you were responsible for creating that blueprint?"

I was beginning to think this chick was as nutty as a bag of trail mix. It only made her more attractive. I've always been attracted to crazy. Scratch that; crazy has always been attracted to me, and I'm too lazy to look elsewhere.

"I don't know what you're talking about, toots," I said. "Seems to me that the two ideas you batted at me are somewhat contradictory. Predestination implies that someone else is pulling the strings. How do I create a blueprint that has already been created?"

Nyla smiled and stubbed her cigarette out in the ashtray.

"It is a mystery, isn't it?" she asked.

The waitress returned and set the Gimlet down in front of Nyla. Nyla handed her a five. The waitress kept the change.

Nyla took a sip of her drink, then set the glass down on the table. She put her sunglasses back on, picked up her drink again, turned the glass over, and dumped the contents onto the table.

"Why did you do that?" I asked.

She smiled coyly.

"I don't know," she answered. "I guess you could say I didn't have a choice. Kinda like Febreezi. Kinda like you."

I was only two drinks in, and I already felt trashed. I couldn't quite grasp the situation that was unfolding in front of me. So I kept drinking.

"Who killed Febreezi?" I asked again.

Nyla closed her eyes and took a deep breath. When she opened them, I detected a note of sadness lingering at the edges.

"Some might say that it was greed that killed him. Others might say it was time. The more literal-minded among us would say that it was Martha."

It made perfect sense, of course. Martha was my connection to Febreezi and the only real suspect. Still, it seemed too clean. The papers reported that Febreezi's office had been ripped apart. Martha simply didn't have the strength.

"I don't think so, babe," I said. "That's not Martha's style. She couldn't tear apart his office like that."

Nyla sighed.

"Everything will be revealed in time, Johnny," she said. "I know that you want to understand the whole story. I wish I could tell you, but I can't. Just know that people are looking out for you. You're necessary. More necessary than you could ever imagine."

"What do you want me to do?" I asked.

"Consider a lawn," she said.

"A lawn?" I asked, confused.

"A lawn. Overgrown with weeds and crabgrass. Lurking somewhere in that lawn is something you need. You can't mow the lawn, for fear that you will tear the thing to pieces. What do you do?"

"I don't know," I answered, puzzled. "You rake it?"

She smiled and patted me on the cheek.

"That's a good boy. Now, you ask me what do you do? The answer is: you rake the lawn. Do not mow. Preserve the lawn."

"What the hell does that mean?" I asked.

"Do what comes naturally, Johnny," she said. "the lawn will take care of itself."

With that, she glided off the seat and into the night. I didn't follow. It didn't seem to come naturally.

15

I didn't much feel like dancing, but I didn't feel safe going back to my apartment, so I went to the Toilet. I parked in my usual spot. The parking lot was unusually empty. Since I'd heard the news about Febreezi that morning, the air had felt strange, like it was ready to coil into a ball at any moment and start the Big Bang all over again.

Rascal, the doorman, felt it too.

"Slow night, Johnny," he said. "People are scared. This whole business with Guy Febreezi has really turned this town upside-down."

"And it's only gonna get upside-downerer," I said.

He nodded and opened the door for me.

The place was practically empty. A few of the regulars were lounging around the booths at the edge of the dance floor, bored. Even the DJ seemed affected. In place of the usual blaring disco music, he was spinning some kind of down-tempo trance beat. Usually, an open dance floor would have drawn me like a magnet, but tonight was a night for drinking, not dancing.

Boris, the regular bartender, was off again tonight. Henry stood behind the bar with his arms folded. When I sat down, he walked over with a big plastic grin on his face.

"Good to see ya', Astronaut!" he said. "Check out those fetish mags like I told ya' to?"

"Didn't have time," I answered. "I'm gonna have to take your word for it."

"Too bad," he noted. "That's some kinky stuff, all right. I never knew Ptsaurians had that many holes!"

"Sounds great," I said, taking a Palmetto out of my pack and knocking it against the bar. "What can you make special for a guy who's had a rough day?"

The bartender paused in consideration.

"Let's see ... what's the ticket for you ..." he said, racking his brain. "You got anything against Cantilever Joy Juice?"

My mouth started to water at the mere mention of the words. Cantilever Joy Juice was among the most potent mixers available on the black market. If Central D. found out you were serving Cantilever, they would shut you down, kick you out, and then throw a party with your supply. I had only had it once at an underground wrestling match on the twelfth moon of Centaurus. I don't remember much of the experience, but somehow I ended up with the championship belt and a headache that lasted well into my early adult years.

"Maybe just a little glass," I said.

He smiled and poured me a double shot of the bright orange liquid.

"Cheers," I said, tipping the glass toward him. I took a sip. The alcohol flowed into my mouth and came alive, waltzing around my tongue like a ballroom dancer. Cantilever had a mind of its own. It went down your throat when it was good and ready to go down.

"So, Astronaut," Henry said, when I had taken another few sips. "I hope I'm not out of line here, but a couple of the guys and I couldn't help but notice you dancing with that Ruskan chick the other night. What gives?"

I shot him the coldest glance I could muster under the influence of the Joy.

"Never mind that," I said. "I was working."

He waved his hands in apology.

"You're right, it's not my place," he said. "I know you've got your business taken care of. Another shot?"

I nodded. "Don't be stingy."

One drink later, I was singing like a canary.

I always had a tough time around bartenders. Something about the environment of a bar made me flap my gums like an eighty-year-old hooker. I knew as soon as I started talking that I was making a mistake. A good P.I. doesn't reveal his cases to anyone. After two glasses of Cantilever, I was not a good P.I..

I told him everything. Starting with the trip back from Aquari, all the way through the meeting with Nyla. It felt good to get it off my chest to an impartial listener. When I was all done, he looked at me and grinned.

"There's something I'd like you to see," he said.

He motioned for me to follow him. I stepped back behind the bar. Funny, as many times as I had been there, I had never been behind the bar. It felt strange, like the magician's secrets were being revealed. I followed him back to the far corner of the bar. We passed through a door that led to a staircase. The room was spinning mildly. I grabbed onto the handrail and followed him down the stairs.

"Just a few more steps," he said.

He led me to a room in the basement. He flipped on the lights.

Seated on a chair in the far corner was Boris, the regular bartender. Something looked different about him. New shoes? Watch? Or could it be that his head was missing?

I turned around and looked at the substitute bartender in shock.

"It's okay, Astronaut," he said. "I'm on your side."

And then everything went black.

16

At the first moment of awareness after an intense sleep, one sometimes feels as though he has no idea where he is. I had that feeling. I guess it's because I had no idea where I was.

I opened my eyes. I shut my eyes. No difference. Wherever I was, it was not well lit. It was not even okay lit. There was no light.

I needed a cigarette. If I could move my arms, I could fix the light situation and the cigarette situation in one fell swoop. I could not move my arms. I shook my arms a little to make sure they still had feeling. They did indeed, and that feeling was pain. My head still had feeling, too—lots and lots of feeling. I may have been blind, but I was not paralyzed.

My hands, I could move. They were behind my back. Not directly behind my back. Something was in the way, and that something was a chair.

As far as I could piece it together, this was the situation: I was bound to a chair in an unlit room. I didn't feel the fabric of a blindfold against my face. I could move my mouth. Whether or not I could produce sound was still up for grabs.

My ears were working just fine. I knew this because I could hear a noise in the room, a noise that I could only classify as a slither. Someone or something was slithering. Maybe several somethings; I couldn't be sure. I didn't have much to go on.

"Isss he awake?" one of the someones or somethings asked.

"Yah, he issss," another someone or something responded.

"Assstronaut," slithered the first slithering something, "isss you awake?"

The voice sounded familiar to me, but I couldn't quite place it.

"I don't know," I said. "I might be dreaming."

Terrifying laughter pealed out around me.

"Thisss isss no dream, Assstronaut," one of the slithering somethings hissed.

"No dream!" shouted another.

"Do you remember ussss, Assstronaut?" one of the slithering somethings behind me asked.

Suddenly, it hit me. There was only one race of people who spoke with such a pronounced hiss: Ptsaurians. And I only knew one group of Ptsaurians; the group that paid me to find their uncle on Aquari. That explained the darkness; Ptsaurians were hypersensitive to light.

The moment of relief that came from knowing who my captors were was quickly superseded by the panic of not knowing what they were going to do.

"You owe usss sssome money, Assstronaut," the first Ptsaurian hissed. That must have been the oldest brother, Xy'gok. When we were back on Aquari, he did most of the talking.

Sometimes, I didn't know when to leave well enough alone.

This was one of those times. Bound to a chair, a man has very few options. The intelligent man realizes that he does not have a lot of power in this situation and agrees to whatever terms the captor presents. I, apparently, was not the intelligent man.

"Why do I owe you money?" I asked. "I did what I was supposed to do. I earned my fee fair and square."

A scaly palm shot out of the darkness and slapped me across the face.

"We were not happy with your performanccce!" Xy'gok shouted. "We did not pay you to find a misssing aunt, we paid you to find a misssing uncle!"

"But," I objected, truly not knowing when to stop, "the missing aunt *was* the missing uncle. It's not my fault he went fruity."

That got the bastards hissing.

"Lemme at him!" screamed the one behind me.

"Me too!" screamed another one behind him.

"Zy'xil!" commanded Xy'gok. "Contain your brothersss!"

A slithery scuffle ensued behind me. I could feel the air whooshing past me as Zy'xil moved to the back of the room. This was my chance. I only had a split second to get my hands free. Luckily, I had been in this situation before and I was prepared. I always kept a tiny knife in my back pocket. While Xy'gok and Zy'xil occupied their selves with their fighting brothers, I reached into my back pocket and cleanly sliced through the ropes that bound my hands.

I took off in a blind run, holding my hands in front of me to make sure that I didn't run into anything. The Ptsaurians noticed immediately that I was free and leapt toward me. I reached into my front pocket and pulled out my lighter. One of them grabbed me from behind. I spun and flicked the lighter to life directly in front of his yellow eyes. He squealed in pain and reeled back as though he had been punched in the face with a brick. I kept the lighter going and waved it around in front of me like a sword. The other three Ptsaurians cringed at the back of the room.

I looked over my shoulder, still holding the lighter aloft in front of me. I was nearly at the door. Next to the door was a light switch. I flicked it on.

The Ptsaurians covered their eyes and fell to the floor, screaming. I flung the door open and ran out into the night.

I was standing in a nondescript alley. I had to get moving, quickly. It wouldn't take long for the Ptsaurians to put on their light-blocking glasses and track me down.

I ran out of the alley and into the street. The wind howled softly across a road completely devoid of cars. To the left, I could see two smokestacks rising from a building into the air. I ran toward them. As I ran, I caught a street sign hanging above an intersection—Pulliver Street. I knew where I was. Pulliver Street ran through Bontemps. The smokestacks sat atop the building formerly known as the Febreezi casino.

I decided it would be a smart move to get out of the center of the road. I ducked into the first alley I came to and scaled the fence at the end. I was sopping with sweat, panting heavily, my entire body ached, and I was in desperate need of a cigarette. Typical day.

I stuck to the shadows as I made my way to the Febreezi factory. The streets were desolate and eerie. Guy Febreezi would have been happy to know how much of an impact his death had made on the community. He probably would have thrown on his queer plaster pants and done a little jig in celebration.

I didn't feel vulnerable until I got to the parking lot in front of the casino. It was only a couple hundred yards across, but it was totally open space in the pitch-black night. If there were any Ptsaurians around, I was a sitting duck.

About halfway across the parking lot, I heard a motor. I took off running. Down the road, I could see a car cloaked in darkness, making its way to the factory. Chances were good that it was the Ptsaurians; any other car would have had its headlights on. There was nowhere to hide. When I actually got to the casino door, there was no guarantee that my odds would improve. Come to think of it, the whole place had probably been sealed down by Central D.

I broke through the police tape in front of the casino and sprinted the last several yards to the factory. The car's tires squealed as it turned into the parking lot. They saw me. I got to the door and tried the handle. Locked. The car picked up speed and headed directly towards me. This was it.

Suddenly, the door flew open. A big, meaty palm grabbed me around the waist and pulled me in.

I was beginning to think the Ape might be all right.

17

"Say Astronaut," the Ape said, once we were safely inside the dark casino, "what's all the hubbub?"

"Got tossed into a pit of vipers," I answered. "And me without a mongoose."

The Ape cocked his head and stared at me, perplexed.

"You got a snake problem?" he asked.

"You might say that."

"I don't care for snakes," he said, shuddering a little.

A loud rapping at the door made us both jump.

"Are those the snakes?" the Ape asked.

I nodded.

"I don't care for snakes," he repeated.

The Ape tossed open the casino door, catching Xy'gok in mid-rap. Xy'gok and his brothers seemed a lot less menacing staring up at the hulking seven and a half foot beast that I was now proud to call my friend. The Ape was nothing if not cordial.

"May I help youse?" he asked.

Although they can be quite rough when they have the upper hand, Ptsaurians are easily intimidated in unfamiliar situations. Xy'gok and the boys cowered before the Ape in fear. I stood silently behind him and tried my best to look tough. As all of my facial expressions have a tendency to do, it probably came across as boredom.

Finally, Xy'gok stepped up.

"We mean you no disssressspect, sssir," he said. "We've come for Assstronaut."

The Ape looked over his shoulder at me.

"You got business with these snakes?" he asked.

"Nothing that wasn't settled a long time ago," I replied.

The Ape turned back to the Ptsaurians.

"Mr. Astronaut says he don't have no business with ya'," he said. "I suggest you and your slimy friends get back into your car and go find some rock on which to bask."

Xy'gok flicked a forked tongue out from between his dried lips. The Ape stood his ground. I stood my ground. The ground wobbled. We managed to hang on.

My side won the staring contest. Without saying a word, Xy'gok and his brothers turned tail, piled into their car, and drove out of my life. Something told me I would see them again.

The Ape shut and locked the door behind them. With shaky fingers, I pulled a Palmetto out of my pack and flipped it toward my mouth. The cigarette bounced off my lips and onto the casino floor. I could never get that trick right.

The Ape crouched down, picked up my cigarette, and handed it to me.

"Thanks, Ape," I said. "That's the second favor you did me tonight. Couple more and you could outdo my parents. You've already done me better than all my friends and my ex-wife."

The Ape stood up and brushed his knees off.

"Geez, Astronaut," he said. "You sure do manage to get yourself into a lot of trouble."

I lit the cigarette that was now dangling between my lips.

"You don't know the half of it," I said. "I could really use a drink."

He gently placed his hand on my shoulder.

"I think that can be arranged," he said. "Come on back to the office. We'll get you fixed up."

I followed the Ape through the rows of silent slot machines, past the dealer-free poker tables, around the motionless roulette wheels, back to the casino offices. A dark, empty casino, I decided, was one of the saddest places in the world. A tear formed at the corner of my eyes. A place that had brought joy to so many people, so unfairly shut down in its prime. Why did the good ones always die so young?

The Ape paused for a moment before opening the door to Febreezi's office. He looked a little choked up, too.

"This is the first time I been in here since ..." the Ape started.

I awkwardly patted him on the back. Sympathy had never been my strong suit. Not the feeling of it, I had that in spades. I could feel sympathy for a paper cut. But the showing of it, that's what tripped me up. I always ended up saying something stupid like, "He probably should have died," or "That's okay, my egg salad sucks, too."

"There, there, Ape," I said. "Guy's in a better place now."

If, by "better place," I was referring to heaven, then I was lying through my teeth. Last I checked, heaven was not real welcoming to lying, cheating, murdering mob bosses. If, on the other hand, "better place" referred to being buried beneath six feet of dirty, then yeah, it probably was a little better than this place. However the Ape took it, it seemed to make him feel a little better.

"Say Johnny," the Ape asked brightly, turning the knob that led into Febreezi's office, "ya' think they got whores in heaven?"

"All the whores you can handle, Ape. All the whores you can handle."

The Ape smiled.

"Mr. Febreezi would like that," he said, holding back a sniffle. "He loved whores like nobody's business."

He flung open the door to Febreezi's office and stepped inside. Say what you would about Central Development, they certainly laid out the cash for the cleaning staff. If I didn't know better, I hardly would have guessed that a brutal slaying had taken place here less than 24 hours prior.

The Ape poured two glasses of bourbon for me, but kept one of them. I tilted my head back and swallowed the shot in one gulp. I had never needed a drink as badly as I did now. At least, not since the last time I needed a drink. It's funny, I never really realized how much I needed alcohol until I became an alcoholic.

When I opened my eyes, the Ape was staring at me expectantly with his glass raised.

"Uh, here's to Guy," I said, clicking my glass to his.

"To Guy," he agreed, solemnly.

I walked over to the bar and examined the bottles lined up across the top. Febreezi knew how to stock a bar. Borzoi Cognac, Desadore Rum, Hastings Whiskey, Floating Pear Chagrine ... I paused with my hand on the bottle of Chagrine, racking my head. Somewhere within my pathetic memory, I remembered Febreezi mentioning the Chagrine the last time I had seen him. I lifted the bottle out of the row and took a closer look at its contents. The back label seemed to be slapped on pretty haphazardly. I peeled the label back slightly. From behind the label, a tiny piece of folded paper dropped out and fluttered to the floor.

Suddenly, a pounding came from the front door, back across the casino floor. The Ape looked at me and shook his head.

"Your snakes don't seem to take a hint very well, Johnny," he said. "Guess I'll have to go teach 'em a little respect."

As soon as the Ape was out of the office, I bent down and picked up the tiny sheet of paper. Across the back, someone, presumably Febreezi, had written the words "Johnny Astronaut." I unfolded the note and read what was written on the inside.

Dear Johnny:

If all has gone according to plan, you are reading this note soon after a rather harrowing experience with a gang of Ptsaurians. I am dead. The Ape has just taken off across the casino to answer a knock on the door. He will not return. You must leave now. You have no choice. Sneak out of the office and take a left down the first row of slots. Take another left at the fountain and head out the back door. Martha will be waiting for you in a car. Get in and tell her to drive you to the safe house as quickly as possible. She knows where it is. No one will think to look for you there.

Everything will be explained in due time. Godspeed and good luck.
Best,
Guy Febreezi
P.S. There is no such thing as luck.

Across the casino floor, a gunshot rang out, followed by a loud crash, a crash that sounded a lot like a 350-pound gorilla hitting the floor.

18

There comes a point in every man's life when he realizes that he no longer has any sort of control over the events that are unfolding around him, when the only things he has left to trust are his instincts. Some might call it an awakening. If this was an awakening, I wondered, why was I so tired?

I ducked out of the office and took an immediate left through the row of slots. Across the floor, I could hear the heavy footsteps of a group of people entering the casino. Whoever owned the feet that were producing the footsteps, one thing was certain: it wasn't the Ptsaurians. Ptsaurians didn't step, they glided. Humans were the only race that clomped like that.

My situation wouldn't allow me to clomp. I had to be quiet and nimble. I breezed through the row of slots, keeping my head low. As the letter stated, at the end of the row, I came to a fountain, where I took a hard left. The footsteps of the Ape's killers reverberated across the casino floor.

I got to the back door, just as the letter said I would, and turned the handle. Right before I slipped outside, I heard a familiar voice yell out my name from across the casino. Against my better judgment, I turned toward the voice.

It was Charvez.

He hadn't seen me. He was calling my name out, expectantly. I wasn't about to give him the pleasure of a response. I snuck through the cracked door and out into the back alley.

Once again, the letter didn't disappoint. Seated behind the wheel of a fabulous new Barclay Détente 3600 (that was most likely paid for with my money) was a woman I thought I knew all too well. I scurried around the other side of the car, opened the door, and climbed in.

"What's this all about, Johnny?" she asked crossly. "Some bastard woke me up and told me that you were in grave danger and I needed to come pick you up. What have you gotten yourself into now?"

"No time to talk, Martha," I said. "Charvez is in there and he's not in the best of moods. Take me to the safe house."

Martha shook her head.

"I don't think so, Johnny," she said. "Not until you explain to me what I'm doing here at two o'clock in the morning."

I handed her the letter. Martha was no dumb chicken, but she was hardly a scholar. I tapped my fingers impatiently against the window as she slowly sounded the words out under her breath.

"Geez Louise!" I finally exclaimed. "I coulda gotten through Moby Dick and a couple of chapters of War and Peace by now! Put your foot on the gas and drive!"

Martha set the letter down on her lap and pursed her lips.

"Honestly, Johnny, this is so like you. You're so impatient. Like that time with the laundry, do you remember? I told you the sheets took a little extra time, but no, you had to have ..."

I glanced out the window next to her and noticed that the doorknob on the back door was shaking. Someone was trying to get out.

I swung my leg around the seat divider, pulled the car into drive and slammed my foot down on top of hers. The car lunged forward and began accelerating down the alley.

"Damn it, Johnny!" she screamed. "You're breaking my foot!"

"That's not the only thing I'm going to break," I said, "if you don't stop acting like a child and drive this damn car."

We were coming to the end of the alley. I was driving the car from the passenger seat. Martha was tensed up against the seat, clucking her tongue at my personal space invasion.

"You're going to get us killed, Johnny," she said, tersely.

"No," I snapped, as the car spun out onto the road. "You're going to get us killed. Now put your damn hands on the wheel and drive."

Martha finally relented to common sense, but she wasn't happy about it. I was sure to get an earful later.

I swung my leg back to my side of the car and collapsed against the seat. I couldn't remember the last time I had fallen asleep without passing out. My entire body was pounding from a combination of stress and a recent history of severe, recurring beatings.

I looked behind us to see if we were being followed. I saw no one. That didn't mean we weren't being followed. For all I knew someone had hitched himself to the bottom of the car. I didn't know anymore. I used to consider myself fairly attentive to these matters, back before reality spun out of control. Back when a dame was a dame and a bottle of shaving cream still lasted a couple of months.

"What did that note mean?" Martha asked. "What's going on?"

"You tell me," I said. "I know about the check. And more importantly, I know that you killed Guy Febreezi. So why don't you come clean and tell Daddy all about it?"

Martha bit her lip, stuck between a rock and another rock. I could see the windmills turning in her mind. They turn pretty quick when you've got a heavy breeze blowing between your ears.

"It was ..." she began, "I was ... I just ..."

"Spit it out, honey," I said. "I've got nothing but time."

Her eyes welled up as she turned to face me. Again, with the weepy peepers. It was getting so I needed to put on a raincoat just to have a conversation with her.

"Oh, Johnny," she sobbed. "You don't know the stress I've been under. I never meant to hurt you, Johnny, honest I didn't. I just wanted to help Guy out. Those bastards at Central Development were bleeding him dry. He just wanted to come clean, to start a new life ... or so he said. I meant to make up for it, honest I did, once Guy and I got settled in our new life together. You see, Johnny, Guy Febreezi and I ... we were lovers."

"Your track record doesn't fail you, dollface," I said. "I guess I should consider myself lucky. Guy Febreezi, you left dead. Me, you just left dead inside."

Martha threw her mouth open and let out a piercing wail. The car began to drift off the road as she closed her eyes and shook with despair against the steering wheel. I grabbed the wheel and steadied us out.

"Watch the friggin' road, you loon!" I shouted.

Martha wiped her eyes and gripped the steering wheel. She stared straight ahead at the empty streets.

"It was all going to be so simple," she said. "Guy came across this book that was worth millions. We just needed some traveling money to get to Ruska, where we were going to sell it. But then Central D. got wind of what was happening and started asking questions. I got scared, Johnny. I didn't want you to be involved. So I went to Guy and tried to get your money back. He told me that he never had any intention of taking me with him; he just needed me to get your money. He pulled a gun on me. He was going to kill me, the rat.

"I knew he couldn't do it, though, not when I went into my hurt little girl routine. I begged for my life. When he drew in closer, I kicked him in the balls, grabbed the gun out of his hand, and blammo. Taught him a lesson he won't forget."

"That's sounds real nice on paper, Martha," I said, "but a couple of things don't make sense. First of all, why did you need to get the money from me? Why didn't you just use the money you had used to pay off my debts?"

"I didn't pay them off, Johnny," she admitted, sniffling. "Febreezi took care of it. He made a deal with Central D. Anyway, he said you wouldn't need the money, because you were going far, far away soon, to a place where your cubits would be worthless."

"Criminy, Martha!" I shouted. "Whaddya mean, you didn't want me involved? Sounds to me like Febreezi was planning on having me killed!"

Martha looked at me, quizzically.

"Think so?" she asked. "I really didn't take it that way. I tried to clear your name, Johnny. I went back the next morning to get the check. Unfortunately, someone else had beaten me to it. They tore apart the office. I don't know why they needed to do that. The check was sitting right on Guy's desk."

"I'll betcha anything it was Central D., Martha, and I'll betcha anything they were looking for the book. If Charvez let me off the hook for nothing, Febreezi must have promised him something sweet."

"That rat!" Martha said, slapping the steering wheel in anger.

"You can say that again," I replied. "What I wanna know is, who has my money?"

"Oh," Martha said, surprised. "That's no mystery. I have your money. I took it back from Febreezi after I shot him."

"Listen, Martha," I said. "You got me into a hell of a mess here. Charvez has the canceled check. He thinks I killed Febreezi. If you really wanna help me, you have to come clean and tell Charvez everything."

"I can't!" Martha said, panicked. "It's too messy! Charvez'll think that I killed him!"

"You did kill him," I said coldly.

Martha burst into a new round of waterfalls.

I was exhausted, dead beat. I looked and smelled like an escaped convict who had been shacked up with a family of baboons. My mind was heavy with the weight of the information Martha had just revealed. If I could just get a little nap, I could think again.

"Stick to the back roads," I mumbled, my eyelids dropping.

Martha grunted something under her breath.

"What did you say, darling?" I asked through a dark, intoxicating fog.

Martha turned to me and sniffed.

"I wish you were dead," she said.

19

... at the Copa
Copacabana
The hottest spot north of Havana
At the Copa
Copacabana
Music and passion were always the fashion at the Copa
Don't fall in love ...

I was twirling Nyla around the dance floor, surrounded by a crowd of Ptsaurians. I spun her into a dip. The Ptsaurians applauded. Above the dance floor, Charvez stood behind a pair of turntables, spinning "Copacabana" at 33 1/3.

At the conga break, I spun Nyla out and let go of her hand. She disappeared somewhere into the crowd. Before I knew it, Martha had taken her place. The dance floor turned into jelly and our feet began to sink.

"I wish you were dead," she said.

"I already am," I answered.

I opened my eyes. We were sitting in the driveway of a dark house, out in the country. Where exactly, I couldn't be sure. Barry Manilow played on the radio. Martha was leaning on the steering wheel, sobbing. My first impulse was to comfort her. My second impulse was to strangle her to death and leave her for the wolves. My third impulse was to get out of the car and walk up to the house, which was the impulse I followed.

I tried the front door. Unlocked. I opened the door and walked in.

"Hello?" I called out. There was no response.

I found a light switch next to the door and flicked it on to reveal a small, sensible living room in what appeared to be a family's house. Batball trophies and photos of smiling children were carefully placed on the bookshelves that lined the room. A worn couch sat against the back wall. In the middle of the floor, a coffee table held old hunting and fishing magazines. In the front, next to the door, a small telescreen sat atop an unvarnished end table. It was cozy. Not the kind of place you'd expect to find a runaway gangster.

I ascended the stairs to the left of the couch and flicked the lights on. I was in a nice-sized sitting room. To the right, a bedroom, and to the left, a kitchen. Behind me, next to the stairs, was the bathroom. It suddenly occurred to me that I hadn't urinated in about 12 hours. And it occurred to me hard.

I rushed into the bathroom and pulled my zipper down. Ah, sweet relief. No matter how beat up a man is, a good pee can still warm the old heart.

As I washed my hands, I looked at myself in the mirror. I appeared to have aged 20 years. My lip was cracked and bleeding from the hit I had taken in the Ptsaurian house. My ribs ached from the Ruskan beat-down at the horse track. An enormous bruise dominated my upper forehead from the time the Ape hit me with the two-by-four. I thought back fondly to the day, just a few days prior, when the Ape and I were brutal enemies. A tear rolled down my cheek. Poor Ape.

When I turned around, Martha was standing in the doorway, looking dejected. A flash of anger erupted inside my brain. If it weren't for Martha, none of this would have ever happened. I would be lying in my bed, cozy as a cucumber, after having tied one on and stunned the dance floor at the Toilet once again. Febreezi and the Ape would still be alive. My face would still look the way it was supposed to and my telescreen would work properly.

Before I could scream at Martha and release some tension, she burst into tears.

"Johnny," she wailed, "Johnny, I'm sorry. I've done a bad thing, Johnny, a horrible thing. You've gotta forgive me. You've gotta hold me, Johnny. You've gotta."

If I could have possibly comforted her less, I would have. I would have leaped at the opportunity to fade into the wall and disappear. Closeness, unfortunately, was dictated by proximity, which was dictated by the tiny bathroom that we were both standing in. I couldn't be farther away from her, but I didn't have to touch her.

It wasn't long before I was touching her. It wasn't long after that before I was kissing her. Shortly thereafter, I had removed her clothes with my teeth and we were lying in the bedroom atop a homemade patchwork quilt that looked as though it had been in the family for generations. After what Martha and I were about to do to it, they wouldn't want it in the family anymore.

What is it about your first love that keeps you coming back for more? I asked myself this question as I savored a post-coital Old-Fashioned. There are those who say happiness can't be found at the bottom of a bottle. I say they're right, because you need several bottles to make a proper Old-Fashioned. I also say that happiness can't be found anywhere else.

Martha and I lay somewhat contentedly atop the old quilt, unaware of our nakedness. A cool breeze blew in the window. Outside, the morning light was just starting to poke its way in through the trees.

"Say, Martha," I asked.

"Yes?" she responded.

"How much do you know about this book that Febreezi was buying?"

"Not too much," she said, scratching herself indelicately. "I know that he was planning on selling it to a group of Ruskans. I think it was some sort of religious text. He said there were only a few copies in existence."

"Say, Martha," I asked again.

"Yes?" she responded.

"Were you planning on killing me?"

Martha sighed.

"No, Johnny," she said. "And I really don't think Febreezi was, either. He said that you were going somewhere far away. I got the impression that he knew something about your future that you didn't."

I tried to put two and two together, but it kept adding up to five. Every answer just opened up a new jar of questions. One thing was certain; I needed to find out more about that book. I needed to

... what was it Nyla had said? Rake the lawn.

The hardest question, to me, was why Febreezi would have written me that note. Could he really have predicted everything that he wrote about? I had once known a girl who worked as a fortuneteller in a traveling carnival. She taught me a trick or two about the business. Enough, anyway, to know that it was all a bunch of hooey. People's reactions can be read, but never the future. Febreezi prophesied exact events. Not only that, they were exact events that occurred at exactly the right moment. How did he know that I would act on my hunch and find that note?

"Martha," I asked, "did Febreezi ever strike you as having psychic powers?"

Martha snorted.

"The only power he had was the power of impotence," she answered.

20

Something strange happens to your brain when you fall into the cycle of paranoia. Most of us could easily surrender to the temptation; there are hints of conspiracy everywhere we turn, in our relationships, in our workplaces, in the news. Part of the reason why I always chose to work alone was to avoid the constant, nagging feeling that someone in my own place of business was trying to undermine everything I did.

A good private investigator avoids conspiracy theories. They're too neat, and real life is messy. The only way to make a conspiracy work is to keep it self-contained. Say, for example, you wanted to knock over a bank. You might have the most brilliant plan in the world, everything about the robbery might go flawlessly, and then you get stuck in traffic for an hour and a half. There is no way to account for everyone and everything.

I was trying my damnedest to avoid paranoia, but it's hard to not be paranoid when everyone has it in for you. Martha seemed unconcerned. She was snoring like a racecar next to me in bed. I could have easily killed her. Just shove a pillow over her face and hold.

I couldn't do it. Killing her would not bring any relief. Besides, she was the only one who had any idea where we were.

I got up from the bed, walked into the sitting room, and dropped onto the couch. Next to the couch, a happy family smiled at a camera. The youngest boy was holding a huge fish. Behind him, his proud parents beamed as the sun shone onto their boat. I wondered who these people were with their perfect life. And what had happened to them? Was I sitting in the home of a dead family? Had they been murdered like Guy Febreezi?

The questions, I decided, would last until after I had slept.

When I woke up, it was dark outside. Martha was out in the kitchen, cooking something that sizzled. I was still naked. I walked out into the kitchen.

"Hi, honey!" she greeted me, cheerfully. "I was just making some pancakes and bacon. Whaddya say?"

I stared at her through half-closed eyelids. For a split second, I imagined that we were still married. I shuddered at the thought.

"Should probably put some clothes on," I mumbled.

"Okay, sugar!" she said. "I found some clothes in the closet that would probably fit you. Why don't you go clean up?"

I nodded and drowsily lumbered into the bathroom. I turned the faucets and hopped into the shower. It felt good. Much needed.

I got out of the shower and tried on the clothes. They fit me well.

I walked back out to the kitchen and sat down at the table. Martha had a heaping plate of bacon and pancakes prepared for me. I was famished.

"Boy, you slept the whole day away," she said. "You just looked so cute, I didn't want to wake you."

I looked up from my plate and fixed a cold stare on her.

"What's with the happy homemaker act all of a sudden?" I asked her.

Martha pouted.

"Aw, Johnny," she said. "I been doing a lot of thinking today. An awful lot of thinking. I been thinking that maybe you and me, we're not so bad together. Maybe this is fate. I still got the money, you know. We could run away together. Get outta here. We could be happy again, Johnny, I know we could."

"Yeah," I said. "Until the sailors started coming into town. Face it, Martha, we don't work. I don't care how much money we've got."

Martha placed her fork down on her plate and sighed.

"I'm sorry to hear that, Johnny," she said. "Because my only other option is to kill you."

She pulled a pistol out from under her robe and pointed it at me. I shoved another forkful of pancake into my mouth.

"Cut it out, Martha," I said, between bites.

She fired the pistol. The bullet whizzed by my ear so close that I dropped my fork.

"Martha," I said, "let's be reasonable about this. Killing me is not going to do you any good."

She shakily kept the gun on me.

"You're the only one who knows about the plan," she said. "You're the only one who knows I've got the money."

"And I'm the only one who's gonna know," I said. "Come on, toots, whaddya think? Who am I gonna rat you out to? I got just as many enemies out there as you have, probably more. If one of us goes down, we both go down."

"You're the only one who's going down, Johnny," she said. "For the first time in years."

I dove under the table as she fired the pistol into my chair. Beneath the table, I grabbed her legs. She fell backwards, hitting her head on the counter and dropping the gun. I scurried out from under the table, grabbed the gun, and jumped onto her chest, pinning her to the ground. She clamped her eyes shut tight, expecting the shot to come at any minute.

"Damn it, Martha!" I yelled. "This behavior has got to stop!"

Her face relaxed as she realized that I wasn't going to shoot her. When she opened her eyes, a stream of old friends were dancing around them.

"I need help," she wailed.

21

Even I couldn't turn down a heartfelt plea for help. I gave her a little bit of what I like to call "bondage therapy." I helped her up off the floor and into a chair, where I helped her let go of her need for control by tying her hands and legs up tight. The great thing about bondage therapy is that you also get to enjoy a little bit of primal scream therapy at the same time. Until the gag goes in, that is.

I was heading back to the city on Route 183. Martha had been kind enough to help me with directions before I left. What a peach. All it took was a couple of good hard stares from my old friends Mr. Smith and Mr. Wesson.

Route 183 soon turned into the Vicious Turnpike, which led directly into the heart of Outer Borzoi. Now I was faced with the daunting prospect of where to go. My home and my office were out, as was Martha's place. By now, Charvez would have realized that Martha and I were nowhere to be found. He probably had so many goons stashed in our places he needed to fit 'em all in with a shoehorn.

I couldn't go back to the Toilet, on account of bartender troubles. The Ptsaurians would find me if I stuck to the streets. The only place I could really think to go was the Good Times bookstore, but that would be closed at this hour.

In the end, I decided there was only one place left for me. The most dangerous place in the world was also the safest. I decided to go to Calcutta's.

I pulled up to Calcutta's and parked against the curb. The empty streets still seemed to be feeling the effects of Guy Febreezi's murder. Usually, on a night like tonight, there would be all manner of junkies and weirdoes hanging out on the sidewalk, using their self-imposed untouchability as an excuse for acting like jerks. Tonight, even the wind seemed afraid to blow.

Inside the bar, it was a different story. The closing of the casino sent a lot of people scrambling out of the woodwork who normally didn't go to Calcutta's. I immediately regretted my choice. The epicenter of the underworld was not the smartest place for a man to be when he was in trouble with the law.

My usual spot was taken by a crowd of one-eyed Mirkens. Mirkens were not a one-eyed race of people, so why this crowd was all wearing eye patches was anybody's guess.

The only seats left were near the bar. Most of Calcutta's customers liked to stick to the tables, in the shadows. When you were at the bar, anyone could come up behind you and knife you in the back. The irony was that at Calcutta's, they were just as likely to knife you in the front. But safety is always an illusion, anyway. You can seal yourself up in a high-rise apartment and never leave and still die of gas poisoning. If you're meant to be gotten, you will be got.

Against my better judgment, I took the seat at the bar. The bartender nodded to me gruffly. I can't describe a gruff nod, but I can tell you beyond a question of a doubt that this was what he gave me. I asked for an Old-Fashioned. He nodded again and slowly poured the drink.

I looked around the bar. I recognized a few of the characters milling around from previous cases. Over by the door was Lenny the Loser. Lenny and I once spent a few days tailing each other on a stolen cars case. Turned out neither one of us had anything to do with it. I hated him, anyway.

To the left, behind me was a gang I'd run into a few times. They called themselves the Sailor Boys. They dressed like they were ready to ship off at any moment, even though none of them, to my knowledge, were actually in the Navy. They didn't have much of an M.O. other than to cause as much damage as possible. Immediately to their right was a crew that used to work the old folks' homes, bilking Grandmas out of nickels by way of property investment schemes. They all wore blazers and talked with thick Boston accents, even though Boston hadn't existed for more than 300 years.

I looked over my other shoulder and noticed a few more people I knew. Captain Portsmith, king of underworld shoe repair. Busty Cousins, a former porn star and current whorehouse queenpin. "Dangerous" Daniel McGowan, a/k/a "the Emo Kid." Earlier that year, I'd spent a night with him and a gaggle of horny bachelorettes that I didn't care to remember and probably couldn't even if I tried.

And then, in the corner, a group that looked vaguely familiar. I couldn't quite place them. As I looked back, one of them caught my eye. He stood up. The rest of them stood up. And then I remembered who they were: the Ruskans from the track.

It was too late to make a break for it. One thing you never wanted to do at Calcutta's was cause a scene. If you were causing a scene, it better be because someone just put a hole in your brain and your synapses were firing against your will. Otherwise, someone would take it upon himself to begin firing against your will.

I tried to appear calm as I raised the Old-Fashioned that the bartender has just placed in front of me to my lips. The Ruskans stepped up to the bar and gathered around me.

"Johnny Astronaut?" one of them said. "You need to come with us."

I gulped down my drink and set it back on the bar.

"You boys don't seem to know a lot in the way of manners," I said. "Can't you see I'm trying to enjoy my drink here?"

The three other Ruskans looked to the one who had spoken. He appeared to be the leader. He was leaning against the bar to my right. Directly in front of me and to the left of the taps was a jar filled with silverware. If need be, I could grab a fork from the jar and jam it into his hand before he knew what hit him.

"Don't stick a fork in my hand," he said. "That's not what's supposed to happen."

I looked at the bartender.

"Another Old-Fashioned, please," I ordered.

The leader seemed to be growing impatient. When I was being pummeled on the ground during our previous encounter, I recalled one of the Ruskans saying that they weren't supposed to hurt me. I hoped they remembered things the same way.

The bartender set my drink in front of me. The other three Ruskans looked to the leader. They didn't seem impatient, just scared.

"Johnny," the leader said. "This is important. No one will hurt you. You must come with us."

"Why should I trust you?" I asked. "Last time I ran into you, you weren't quite so chatty."

The Ruskans exchanged worried glances.

"That was Zoni," the leader said. "He's impulsive. He saw you and he got excited. It won't happen again. We have big things to tell you, if you would only come with us. Big things."

I looked into his face. Every private investigator worth his salt in shakers knows the basics of reading faces. I detected a note of sincerity in his expression. I also detected a note of fork in the silverware jar.

I slammed my second drink down, blinked my eyes, and turned toward the leader.

"All right," I said, against my better judgment. "Let's go."

The leader smiled. His goons patted me on the back.

"You won't regret this," he said.

"I don't regret anything," I said. "Everything happens for a reason, right?"

The Ruskans exchanged amused glances.

"That's the truth, brother," the leader said.

22

I followed the Ruskans out to their car, which was parked behind Calcutta's. Someone had shelled out a lot of bucks for the ride. Whoever these Ruskans were, they were connected.

"You may ride shotgun," the leader said.

"Hell no," I responded. "I'm not going to sit up front, where one of your goons can pop a cap in my skull. I'm taking the back, Jack. Next to the door. And it better not be one of those doors that locks from the outside."

The Ruskans exchanged another round of amused glances amongst themselves.

"Whatever you want, Johnny," the leader said.

Two of the Ruskans crawled into the back seat. I followed them. The leader sat in the passenger seat. One of the other three drove. I hoped it wasn't Zoni. I heard he was impulsive.

The driver started the car and the stereo leapt into action. The most beautiful sound that ever existed came out of the speakers, a sound I knew all too well. It was the Bee Gees singing "More Than a Woman" from the Saturday Night Fever soundtrack. The driver looked back at me and smiled.

"Good choice," I said.

The Ruskans nodded.

I turned to the Ruskan next to me.

"Where are we going?" I asked.

The Ruskan looked at me, then looked down into his lap, barely stifling a smile. I couldn't say for sure, but it appeared to be a giddy smile, the kind of smile that I had on my face back when I met Karen Jamey at the Ultrabar. I tried the lock on the door. It worked from the inside.

"I can't say for sure," he said to his lap.

The leader turned around and smiled.

"I would just like to say," he began, "that we are honored to have you with us today, Mr. Astronaut."

"Honored to be here," I said.

They were certainly being a lot more polite this time. It was an interesting approach. Make someone feel welcome and then slice his throat.

"Do you think there's such a thing as concrete truth in the universe, or is reality just a messy ball of shared fictions?" blurted out the one on the opposite end of the back seat from me.

The leader shot him a look that could kill daggers.

"I'm sorry," the one on the opposite end said, looking down at his lap.

We rode the rest of the way in silence. After awhile, my muscles began to relax, which was the first sign that I needed to tense up. Don't get too comfortable with the enemy, I told myself.

My muscles tensed up on their own when I realized where we

were headed. Right on Cantilever, left on Montgomery ... I had traveled this route just a few days ago, in my pursuit of Nyla. We were going to the Good Times Bookstore. Was there a connection, or was it just a coincidence?

We pulled up in front of the store. The driver parked the car and turned off the engine. The leader turned around and smiled at me. I was getting a little tired of all this smiling.

"We're getting out now," the leader said.

"I see that," I responded.

The other Ruskans burst into laughter. "He sees that, of course he sees that!" the one on the opposite end said.

I stepped out of the car. The Ruskans followed me. If I was going to make a break for it, now was the time. I glanced over at the leader, who smiled broadly. Something was awfully strange about these cats. On a previous job, I had been hired to infiltrate a religious cult called the Drennons to kidnap the daughter of a prominent politician. The Ruskans had that same strange look in their eyes that the Drennons had. I felt as though I was being led to the slaughter. Unfortunately, I was out of other options. If I was going to the slaughter, at least I'd be wearing my comfortable shoes.

"Let's go in, shall we?" the leader asked.

"Yep," I said.

The leader went up to the door and knocked three times, rapidly, then a fourth time, more slowly, and then slapped his open palm against the door. This was probably the signal to let his goons inside know that we were coming in. They were probably sharpening their knives, getting ready to pounce.

Another Ruskan came to the door. The leader exchanged a few quiet words to him that I couldn't quite make out. I don't speak

Ruskan, anyway. The Ruskan at the door peered out into the darkness. When his eyes focused on me, he broke into a wide-mouthed grin. I decided that I could get used to this kind of treatment. Most times, when people looked at me, they looked like they'd been sucking lemons.

The Ruskan at the door waved me in. I stepped up hesitantly.

"Come in," he said. "We've been waiting for you."

"All I've been waiting for is death," I answered. "I've got a feeling he's about to find me."

The Ruskan at the door threw back his head and let out a roar of laughter that made me jump.

"Oh, that's rich," he chuckled. "Do come in."

I turned to look at the other three Ruskans behind me. They were still wearing their plastic grins. They all nodded in unison, as though their heads were attached to a single string that was being worked by a one-handed puppeteer.

I let out a deep sigh and walked into the dark bookstore.

The leader lit the path in front of us with a flashlight.

"Follow me, Mr. Astronaut," he said. "It's not far now."

As we walked past the stacks of books and magazines in the pornography section, I took note of some of the titles. *Hardly Gentle Magazine. The Ins and Outs and Ins and Outs of Molly McBride. Awesome Bosoms.* I seriously hoped that this wasn't some kind of bizarre sex cult that I was being led to. I had heard about the Ptsaurian fetish mags in this place.

We walked through the store on the same circuitous path that I took when I had followed Nyla. We headed to the sci-fi section, in the back of the store, straight to the same aisle where I lost Nyla a few days prior.

"Are you ready?" he asked.

To be murdered? I thought.

"Yep," I said, coolly.

He reached up and pulled a book down from the shelf. I heard a whirring noise behind us. I turned around. A sliding panel had opened in the wall.

"That's a neat trick," I said. "Can you set that up in my apartment?"

He chuckled.

"If all goes well," he said, "you won't ever have to worry about your apartment again."

"Sounds ominous," I replied.

"Not ominous," he answered, "promising."

I followed the leader down a dark set of stairs. Behind me, the other Ruskans whispered important-sounding sentences to each other in Ruskan. Everything in Ruskan sounded important, though. For all I knew they were talking about their laundry.

The stairs led to a door on which Ruskan letters were written.

"What does that say?" I asked the leader.

"It says 'Door,'" he answered.

"Right," I said. "In case you forget what it is."

The Ruskans behind me giggled like a bunch of hyenas.

"Shut up!" the leader shouted at them, and the giggling stopped.

"Now, Mr. Astronaut," he continued, "before we go through this door, I need you to understand one thing. You are about to learn secrets that few men on Earth know or understand. The things that you will learn behind this door are going to completely change your perception of reality. You will not be the same person after you have this experience. All I ask of you is that you keep an open mind, you listen to what we have to say, and you try to believe us. I say all of this to you knowing that you're going to be okay. I know how this ends."

I didn't need much more proof than that to know that I was, in fact, dealing with a cult. I had heard that speech before, when I was shacked up with the Drennons. Unbeknownst to the Ruskans, I had been through intense willpower training in my years at detective college. They couldn't break me, no matter how hard they tried. I prepared myself for the worst and hoped for the best.

"I would like to hear you say that you agree," he said.

"I agree," I answered.

"Good," he said. "Let's go in."

He opened the door. I braced myself and stepped inside. Like much of life, it was an anticlimactic experience. I was in a small, windowless room. There were no shrines or podiums or any of the things that one would expect to see in the headquarters of a secret cabal. Seven or eight hard-backed chairs were scattered around the room. In the corner, a small stereo played a song that I forgot I knew. The walls were adorned with old posters and newspaper clippings. I walked over to one of the clippings and read the date: June 4th, 2003. Next to it hung a poster for a film that I'd never heard of called *From Justin to Kelly*. I checked the release date—again, 2003. I tried to remember back to history class. What happened in 2003? I came up blank.

"Johnny?"

A familiar voice rang out behind me. I turned around and confirmed my suspicions. Nyla stood in the doorway. She looked beautiful. As her liquid eyes focused upon mine, it was all I could do to stop myself from running up and planting a passionate kiss upon her lips.

"Johnny?"

Beside her, a figure stepped out of the shadows, and my passion quickly subsided.

Standing beside her was a man I'd come to know all too well and trust all too little—Henry, the bartender/security guard/porn aficionado/major league rat.

23

I checked my front pocket to make sure my gun was still in place. I had a feeling that I might have to leave this bookstore shooting.

"You won't be needing that," Henry said.

"My wallet?" I asked.

"Your gun," he replied.

I warily eyed the pair standing in front of me. Both of their faces were plastered with the same idiot grins as the rest of their crew. Behind them, the others stood, locked in mutual plastic happiness.

"What am I to make of this?" I finally asked.

Henry smiled.

"Have a seat, Johnny," he said, "and we'll explain everything."

I pulled up one of the hard-backed chairs and sat down. The rest of the crew gathered around me.

"Are we going to have a sing-along?" I asked.

The room exploded with unsettling laughter.

"Just like it says!" one of the Ruskans in the back shouted.

"Every word of it!"

"And that as well!" replied another Ruskan.

They pointed at each other and fell into a new round of hysterics.

"Listen," I finally broke in, "let's cut the crap. If you're going to kill me, kill me. If you have something to say, say it. I'm tired of wasting my time with you bunch of jabbering baboons."

Henry wiped a laughter tear from his eye.

"As well you should be, Johnny, as well you should be," he said. "I guess it's time, yes?"

He looked at Nyla who looked back at him and nodded. They both turned to face me.

"Maybe I should have Nyla begin," he said.

"What maybe?" she asked, as the baboons in the back stifled a new round of laughter.

Nyla pulled her chair up close to mine and put her hand on my leg. I don't know what she was wearing, but she smelled like a fresh spring day. I tried to imagine what a stale spring day would have smelled like. I couldn't come up with anything.

Nyla stared deep into my eyes, and instantly, the rest of the room and the rest of the world and the past and the future all melted away.

"Now, Johnny," she said. "I'm going to try to explain something to you. I don't have a sweeping thesis statement or a particular sentence that will make it all make sense. I'm just going to try to tell you what I know. I have been preparing for this moment my entire life, but I don't know what I'm going to say. I'm not allowed to know."

She turned to face Henry, and the spell was broken.

"Remarkable," he nodded.

She turned back toward me and the spell was back on.

"You may ask questions as we go along, if there's something you don't understand. I won't fault you if you don't believe me at first. It is a difficult thing to digest."

"Give me something," I pleaded with her. "Please. Just tell me what's going on."

"Okay," she smiled. "I'm going to show you something, something you've been waiting a long time to see."

My initial hunch was correct; this was some kind of crazy sex thing. But now that I knew Nyla was involved, I wasn't quite so scared.

She reached her hand out, and Henry placed a tattered paperback into it. She handed the book to me in turn. I looked down at the cover. The name of the book was *Johnny Astronaut*.

"It's all about you," she said.

I blinked.

"Do you mind if I smoke?" I asked.

Titterings from the background.

"Not at all, Johnny," she said. "Get comfortable."

I pulled the pack of Palmettos out of my inside suit pocket. Last one. Was that symbolic, or was it just something that happened? I lit my cigarette and blew the smoke out of the side of my mouth to avoid getting smoke into Nyla's beautiful eyes.

"So," I said. "This book, *Johnny Astronaut*. Who wrote it?"

"It was written by a man named Rory Carmichael," she said. "He's unimportant. He's just a writer, a writer who got sucked into a force he couldn't control."

"I see," I said. "And what's it about?"

"It's about you," she said. "It's about everything. From the time you flew back from Aquari to the time the book was written, which will be in the past, which is, perhaps, another thing we should discuss."

"Wait just a good minute," I said. "How did you know I was on Aquari? How long have you been watching me? Are the Ptsaurians in on this?"

I looked at Henry, and suddenly it all made sense.

"You set me up," I said. "It was you, all along. You were there at the bank when I deposited my money. You were the one who introduced me to Nyla. You let the Ptsaurians kidnap me. You killed Boris, and now you're going to kill me."

Henry shook his head.

"No, Johnny," he said. "It's not like that at all. You see, I've known what was going to happen for a long, long time. I read this book, as did my father before me, as did his father before him. I had to be involved, you understand. I had to kill Boris, because the text dictated it. The Ptsaurians, that was a total surprise. Well, I shouldn't say it was a total surprise, because I knew that it was going to happen. But taken contextually ... I had nothing to do with it."

"I know it's hard to understand, Johnny," Nyla said. "I have had many years to prepare for this. When I was just a little girl, the Ruskans came to my home and explained to me the story of *Johnny Astronaut*. I was never allowed to read the book, for fear that my personal choices would influence my actions. No one knows what would happen if the narrative were disrupted. The entire universe could be destroyed."

"Yeah," I said, blowing my smoke directly into her eyes, "the universe would collapse if some crap narrative to some crap book about me were to be disrupted. I don't get you people. You've obviously put a lot of time and energy into your little book club here. What does it get you? You're fighting to defend the right for an insignificant book that I've never even heard of to exist? You turned my entire world upside-down because of a piece of fiction?"

"Your life is the fiction, Johnny," Henry said. "We are powerless to stop it."

"So how much of my life is in this book?" I asked.

"Just recent events," Henry answered. "I don't know, he might have written more. There is room left for a sequel."

"And what did Guy Febreezi have to do with all of it?"

"Aah, Febreezi," Henry said, sadly.

"Febreezi," the Ruskans chanted, shaking their heads.

"Febreezi was ostensibly working for us, Johnny. I say 'ostensibly,' because for all appearances, he did exactly what he was supposed to do. What he was supposed to do, however, was not what he intended to do, but what was necessary, nonetheless."

"I don't understand," I said, cocking my head and blowing smoke into the air. "Was he working for you or wasn't he?"

"It's complicated, Johnny. You see, few people have ever heard of your book. There are only two copies in existence. We have one. For hundreds of years, one of the copies has been passed down in our, as you call it, book club. Febreezi somehow managed to track down the second copy. He read the book, and, understandably, had a lot of questions.

"We knew that he had read the book, because I am telling you right now that he had read the book. So we met up with him, and we explained to him his role in the narrative."

"But I'm confused," I said. "Why would Febreezi go along with it if he knew he was going to die?"

"It's a pretty big load to swallow," Henry admitted. "For you and for Febreezi. He knew that he was destined to die. But Johnny, people don't understand destiny. He thought that he could outsmart destiny and play both sides against the middle. He didn't understand that he was powerless against the narrative, and even if he had understood, he would have been powerless against the narrative."

"Play both sides against the middle, powerless against the narrative ... what do you mean?"

"I mean that everything he did to resist the narrative ended up being exactly what the narrative required. He never intended to die. He intended to run a major double-cross on Central D., Martha, you, and us. A quadruple-cross, if you will. He thought he could steal your money and travel back in time himself, all while keeping up the appearance of playing our game. He was very thorough. He wrote out his little prophetic note and left it on the bottle of Chagrine, just as we told him to. Little did he know that everything he did was predestined to happen exactly as it happened, and all of his struggles against the happening were the happening themselves."

"So where does human will come into the equation? Why do you need to work at all? If everything ends up exactly as it does in the book, why get involved in this long, convoluted plan?"

"It makes for interesting reading," Henry answered.

"Okay, so then, how much is real life and how much is in the book?" I asked.

"It's all in the book," Henry said.

"Well, how was it supposed to happen? If Febreezi knew I was going to steal the book, how did he know that I wouldn't read it?"

"It's all in the book," Henry responded. "The book is it. It is the beginning, the middle, and the end. There are things that are not in the book. It's not a second-by-second chronicle of your every thought and movement. But the basics are all there, exactly as they happened, exactly as they will continue to happen until the book is written."

"All right," I said, "I think I'm with you so far. But I don't quite understand this thing about the book not having been written."

"This was a little tricky for me, too," Nyla said. She turned to Henry. "Do you mind if I try to explain?"

"You don't have a choice," Henry said. The Ruskans nodded.

"The book was written in the year 2003," Nyla told me. "It was written by Rory Carmichael after we paid a visit to him and explained the story. We have to go back in time and make sure that the story will be written, or else …"

"The entire universe could collapse," I finished.

Henry nodded.

"Well, that's where you've got me, toots," I said. "I don't believe in time travel."

"I know," Henry responded.

"Of course you do," I said.

"Here's the beautiful thing, Johnny," Nyla jumped in. "You don't have to believe in time travel. All you have to believe in is disco."

I'll admit, my ears perked up.

"Go on," I said.

"Many centuries ago, our forefathers in the book club discovered that there was one major portal for time travel in Outer

Borzoi, where you would come to live," answered Henry. "That portal is located at the exact center of the dance floor at the Toilet. To open the portal, you must engage in a specific combination of dance moves, which Nyla will teach you. The portal can only be opened during a lunar eclipse. The eclipse is happening tomorrow night."

"Well," I said, "I don't know about opening any time-traveling portals, but I do like to disco."

"Yeah, he's good," Nyla agreed.

"One thing is bothering me," I said.

"What role does Charvez play in all of this?" Henry asked. "We don't know, entirely. Some scholars say that Febreezi must have offered them the book in exchange for excusing your debts, under the assumption that if they actually managed to get their hands on the book, he would be safe in the past and the book would be worthless. Other scholars debate this, saying that the 50,000 cubits would be worthless in the past as well, so obviously his motivation could not have been financial. No one really knows for sure. Most books do not entirely hold up under careful scrutiny.

"We do know that Central Development has eyes in places none of us know about. They could know everything, or they could know nothing, depending on which eyes they're choosing to look through at the time."

"I thought you knew everything," I said.

"Not everything," he answered. "But I can tell you this for certain; Charvez smells something funny coming from your direction, and you'd be wise to be on the lookout for him. Even a man of strong faith like myself still has a modicum of doubt. From this moment on, anything is possibly possible."

Henry stood up from his chair.

"And now, I must be going," he said. "You have until tomorrow night. Nyla is going to take you to a safe place where no one will bother you and teach you the combination. It's going to be hard work, but I have a lifetime of faith that has only recently been proven worthwhile. Just remember, Johnny: don't mow. Rake."

He turned his back on me. The Ruskans stood up and began shuffling out the door.

"Just one more question, before you leave, please," I said, as he stood in the doorway.

"Anything," he called out over his shoulder.

"How does it turn out?" I asked.

Henry smiled.

"We're here, aren't we?" he answered.

"That's debatable," I said.

24

Nyla and I rode silently through the city in the Barclay Powercruiser that Henry provided for us. A pounding rain fell from the sky and struck our vehicle, reminding us that we were still in reality and rain was still rain. As we passed by buildings that had always seemed familiar to me, I thought about destiny, and about the many ways that I was planning on ravishing Nyla's beautiful body the minute I got her alone.

    I tried as best I could to reconstruct the events that led up to the conversation in the bookstore, but I kept getting snagged on the little details. If this kooky time travel scheme were to go off as planned, I would have to place a lot of faith in both a group of people who I knew practically nothing about and a concept that I had always assumed to be impossible. Even now, as I sat in the passenger seat thinking about the contortions I was about to put Nyla's body through, I realized that she was a complete stranger to me. And what if (and this was a big what if) what if this was all true, that we really were all characters in some crap novel? Would I have to spend the rest of my life hundreds of years in the past? Did I have a choice in the matter?

"Do I have a choice in the matter?" I asked her.

Nyla wrinkled her brow.

"Choice ... I don't understand," she said.

"Choice," I answered. "Personal preference. Can I walk away?"

"Oh," she said, staring straight ahead through the rain-soaked windshield. "You could walk away. Yes, you could decide we were a bunch of creeps and escape from the car at the next stoplight, if you so choose. But where would you go? There are a lot of people out there who are interested in seeing the end of your existence."

We stopped at a red light and she turned to face me.

"Besides," she said, with a hint of a smile at the corners of her lips, "I don't want you to go."

Damn those eyes, and damn the face that they resided in, and the head that surrounded that face, and the long, graceful neck that propped up the head, and the elegant, feminine shoulders that led into her uncommonly perfect rack and tight little stomach. Damn that petite ass. Damn her short but lithe legs. Damn her stupid, crazy book club, damn her troublesome ethnicity, damn her stimulating accent, and damn her intoxicating perfume.

And damn me, I thought, as the light turned green, for being such a sucker.

We pulled up to a nondescript, rundown building on the corner of Kent and Broadway in the Plastics District. As far as I knew, the Plastics District was not zoned for residential apartments.

Wherever we're going, I thought, there had better be a bed.

We stepped out of the car. Instinctively, I reached for my pack of cigarettes, but then remembered that I had smoked the last one at the bookstore.

"Say, Nyla," I said, "do you happen to have a cigarette?"

Nyla shook her head and wrinkled up her nose.

"It's a filthy habit. You're going to die of cancer if you keep smoking, you know," she said.

I nodded.

"Probably so," I said, "but I'm about to go into a very stressful situation, and this is not the best time for me to be having a nic fit."

She sighed.

"Check the glove compartment," she said. "I'm pretty sure Henry prepared for this."

I opened the door and popped open the glove compartment. Inside sat two full boxes of Palmettos.

"My brand," I said. "Thanks, Henry."

As I shut the glove compartment, I noticed for the first time that someone had taped a note to the door. I ripped it off and held it up to the light. It read:

You're welcome. -Henry

"Let's go!" Nyla shouted. "I'm getting rained on."

We ran to the nearest building, just across the street. Nyla fumbled with a jingling key ring, searching for the one sheet of metal that was cut into the proper shape. She finally found the correct key and stuck it in the lock. The lock made that satisfying 'click' sound that locks make when they're unlocked. She opened the door and we stepped inside.

"It's on the second floor," she said. "Let's walk."

The vast, cold building struck at us like needles as we trudged up the stairs to the second floor. We were both soaked and shivering from the freezing rain. I felt as though I was about to shake my arms off. Nyla's teeth chattered as she fumbled with the keys again.

She found the right key, the lock made the satisfying 'click,' and we stepped into our temporary home.

She flipped on a light switch next to the door. The lights came to life, illuminating a gorgeous dance studio surrounded by giant mirrors.

"A person could have a lot of fun in here," I said, "and not just dancing."

"Come with me," she said. "There's a bedroom in the back. I don't know about you, but I'm freezing."

"And how," I said. "I'm colder than an Eskimo's mother-in-law."

Our footsteps echoed off the walls as we crossed the dance floor to the back room. Nyla opened the door. It was cozy. Just enough room for two people and a half-gallon bucket of lubrication.

Nyla reached into the closet and pulled out two pairs of sweatpants and t-shirts. She handed one of the pairs to me.

"Here," she said, "put these on."

I threw my arm around her back and pulled her close to me.

"I'm going to need some help getting my wet clothes off," I said, staring into her two whirlpools of shimmering stardust, and then looking up into her eyes.

She smiled nervously.

"We're supposed to be dancing," she said.

"There's always time for disco," I said. "Let's take some time to get to know each other."

I leaned down and put my mouth to hers. Her lips were soft yet firm, like a ripe peach without the stubble. Her hands shook from the chill as she slowly worked her way down from my top button to the bottom. I pulled her wet blouse up over her head. There was that awkward moment that always occurs when you're lifting someone else's shirt off and you hit a snag on her head and she's stuck with the dilemma of pulling the shirt off herself or giving in and letting you puzzle your way through it. To Nyla's credit, she let me do the work.

She slipped my shirt and jacket off and began kissing my chest. I didn't know if I was shivering from the cold or from the anticipation. Both were equal parts painful and pleasurable.

We locked our lips in a passionate kiss and eased onto the bed. Our hands began moving in a frenzy of activity as we struggled with the clasps and bindings that were keeping us from being completely natural. My lips never left hers as we removed our slick clothing and introduced our bodies to one another.

I had never felt such intense sensual pleasure. Martha was a hoot, don't get me wrong, but this was more than a lark. This was what it was supposed to feel like, the act of giving yourself to another entirely. I decided at that moment that whatever crazed idea she had about disco dancing our way into the past, I would follow. Whatever happened, I could not handle living the rest of my life without her.

Shortly afterwards, I began to have doubts again.

I lay on my back, smoking a cigarette. She was cradled on top of me, under the covers. I blew smoke rings into the air and waited for the moment when we could move on to the next phase.

"We should dance, baby," I said, planting a subtle kiss on her forehead.

"Mmm," she answered.

"Are you falling asleep?" I asked.

"Mmm," she answered.

I threw my arm to the side and stubbed my cigarette out on the end table next to the bed.

"I guess I am, too," I said.

25

When we awoke the next afternoon, a soft light was resting comfortably on the bed covers. It wasn't until I cleared the crust from my eyes that I realized I hadn't had a single drink the evening before. So this was what it was like to wake up sober. A person could get used to this. Or a person could have another drink. I wondered if there was any alcohol in the studio.

Nyla yawned and stretched her legs. Her body shivered the way a cat shivers after a good day's sleep. She wet her lips with her tongue and opened her eyes to look at me, a contented smile alighting her face. "What time is it?" she asked, in a groggy early-morning voice.

I looked at my watch.

"4:30," I said.

Her eyes suddenly popped wide open and she sat bolt-upright in bed.

"4:30?" she asked, frantic. "4:30? We don't have any time! Damn it, Johnny! We only have five hours before we're supposed to meet Henry and the others at the disco! That's not enough time to learn an entire combination!"

I shook a cigarette out of the pack and lit it up.

"Relax, baby," I said. "We're living on fiction time, now. If it's happening, it happened, and it's happening, so relax, dig? I think, instead of learning the dance, you should let me show you a couple of combinations I learned in the whorehouses on Planatron."

Nyla pursed her lips together in an expression that was eerily reminiscent of my long-suffering ex-wife. She grabbed the cigarette from between my lips, threw it on the hard floor next to the bed, and gave me a mighty shove. I tumbled off of the bed and onto the floor, nearly knocking myself a new eyehole on the bedside table.

"What gives, ya' dingbat?" I shouted. "I thought we were playing nice!"

As she stood over me in the buff, her tight little body stern as a schoolmistress, I couldn't help but get aroused. She looked down at my rising force and grimaced.

"You better put that thing away before you hurt yourself," she said.

"You got a place for me to put it?" I asked.

"Yeah, smart guy," she sneered. "Stick it in your hat. We've got some dancing to do."

"C'mon, babe," I said, propping myself up on my elbow. "Just one more tumble. I can't go into this thing with any regrets."

"What does it take to get through to you?" she asked. "The entire universe is in jeopardy and all you can think about is your wang-dang-doodle."

"Naw," I replied. "It's my wang-dang-doodle that can't stop thinking about me."

"We have more important things to think about than sex right now," she said.

"Yeah, yeah," I answered. "Tell it to Dr. Brody."

"Who the hell is Dr. Brody?"

"I don't know," I said.

She gave me a final look of disgust, then padded down the hall to the bathroom. I looked down at my tent pole and frowned.

"What're you looking at?" it asked me.

After bidding a fond farewell to our nakedness, we were ready to hit the dance floor and begin learning the dance that would save the world. The plan, as Nyla explained it, was for the rest of the crew to arrive at the disco at about 9:00. Henry would keep an eye out for potential trouble at the bar and the Ruskans would infiltrate the disco booth. By the time Nyla and I arrived at 9:30, the Ruskans would be securely in place to spin the necessary song. As soon as we heard the opening bars of "Whistle Bump," we were to make our way to the center of the floor. Four bars in, the routine would begin, and as soon as we hit our final freeze, we would be whisked back in time to the year 2003.

The whole scenario still sounded kooky to me, but I didn't care. For once, I was in a place where I didn't have to be looking over my shoulder every two seconds for the guy who was about to whack me with a lead pipe. I felt comfortable dancing with Nyla in that studio, as though it was exactly where I was meant to be. We could've carved ourselves out a nice little existence there, giving dance lessons to little candy-eating freaks in tutus. Or, we could save the universe from collapsing in upon itself. I was flexible.

For the next three hours, we danced nonstop, going over and over the steps until they started to come natural. It felt good to have a partner who understood me. Most of the time at the Toilet I'd just dance with whatever gin-soaked floozy was available that night. I thought back to the first time I met Nyla, how our instincts played off of each other so eloquently. Like a well-trained batball team, she filled in my weaknesses with her strengths and vice versa. The passion of the disco flowed through our arms and legs as we spun around the hardwood floor together. So different from my relationship with Martha. Dancing with Martha was like trying to pull a donkey with a cart ... you ended up with nothing but a stalled cart and a pissed off donkey.

Panting and heaving, we wove our bodies into a tapestry of finely tuned, subtly choreographed strokes, like music made flesh. Now in each other's arms, now out, now gliding across the smooth floor on feet like greased butter. The wanting, man, the agony and beauty of almost-there-but-not-quite, the steady rhythm of the beat that slid into the ear and out the crotch. That was disco to me. My loins were afire with anticipation. The more we practiced, the cleaner the dance became, the crisper the movements, the more desirous I became, until finally, on the stanza of what was to be our final repetition, I cried out, "Take me, Nyla! Take me! My passion is such that I can bear it no longer! I must have you, my darling!"

Nyla slid into the final pose and leaned against me in position, one hand lightly brushing against my waist, the other placed on the floor, holding her up.

"Save it for the Toilet, Thoreau," she said. "We'll get our kicks in Twenty Aught Three."

It was seven o' clock, and we needed to get ready. As Nyla padded off to the shower, I opened the closet to inspect our clothing options for the evening. Henry had been kind enough to provide us with a full disco wardrobe, and it was hot. I mean, not just sparkplug, but entire freakin' *carburetor*. For Nyla, he had picked out a delicious, red, low-cut, mid-length number, sparkles and sequins bursting off of it like bullets from a dazzle ray. When the disco ball hit that sucker, daddy, she was gonna blind the glasses off of every cat in the joint. But it was the accents that really killed. Instead of a necklace, he had provided her with a slim satin ribbon with a rose clasp—subtle enough to resist claims of tackiness but noticeable enough to draw attention to her long, dark neck and ample bosom. The high-heeled shoes that laced up to just above the ankle were sure to accentuate her trim calves beautifully. I couldn't wait to see it on her.

The outfit he'd left for me made my silver suit look like a cheap piece of junk. The most important night in the history of disco was upon us, baby, and the name of the game was leisure. The suit coat and pants were 100% authentic 1978 polyester, in a brilliant royal blue that shimmered and changed colors in the light. The suit practically danced on the hanger all by itself. I could just imagine what it would look like when we were out on the floor. The wide lapels on the jacket provided a beautiful base for the even wider collar on the sparkling white shirt that peeked out from underneath. The pants were cut perfectly to my body: tight at the top, slowly looser as they went down, ending in a couple of flares that could have saved some lives during nighttime road construction. Tie? Forget about it. This wasn't the supper club, Jack. Instead, I had a gold rope that was thick enough to do some serious mountaineering.

Even if this whole thing didn't go off as planned, I would die a happy man knowing that I had spent a night dancing with a gorgeous lady, both of us dressed like a million cubits.

Nyla returned from the shower, a towel covering all of the naughty parts that I was desperately aching to view. I threw my arm around her shoulders and pulled her up to me, inching a finger under the tightly wound towel. She pulled away and gave me a bewitching smile.

"Someone needs a cold shower," she said.

"It'll fit in perfectly with the cold shoulder I just got," I answered. "From you."

"That probably could've been worded better," she said.

"I didn't write it," I replied.

26

In an act of mercy (or torture, depending upon your perspective), Nyla allowed me to watch her get dressed. I sat in the corner of the bedroom and crossed my legs as she snuggled into her shimmering dress and shoes. Although it was excruciating, I knew that the tension would be good for the dance. By nine, we were dressed and ready to go. Nyla's hot red outfit fit her better than I could have imagined, and I can imagine a lot, daddy-o.

We said goodbye to the dance studio and headed out to the car. Although I felt pretty confident about the dance steps, I was nervous for the night ahead. There were a lot of things that could go wrong. Or maybe there weren't. I tried not to think too hard about the potentials for paradox.

The rain had cleared up and it was a beautiful night. A full moon hung low in the sky, illuminating the dirty city. The corner of the moon was just beginning to be covered by the sun in the opening stages of the eclipse that was to propel us back in time. Nyla handed me the keys. "You drive," she said. I nodded.

I pulled out of the parking spot and headed toward the northern bound Vicious. The streets were more full than they had been lately, the city finally beginning to recover from the death of its prodigal slime. The gang violence that everyone predicted had never occurred, proving perhaps that the only thing that can be predicted is the past.

I looked in the rearview mirror. In the distance, a pair of headlights trailed behind us. I looked over at Nyla, who returned a warm smile. I looked back in the rearview and noticed the other pair of headlights inching significantly closer. A sinking feeling welled up inside of me. We were being followed. More than followed, we were being overtaken.

"Hold on, baby," I said, "we've got a friend back there."

Nyla turned around and looked out of the back window.

"Who is it?" she asked.

"I don't know," I replied, "but I'm gonna try to lose him."

The other car was almost upon us. At the next corner, I suddenly slammed on the gas and took a hard right. Nyla watched out the back as the car sped straight forward, missing the turn.

"Say, Johnny," she said, "I think that's your car. Who do you think is driving?"

"I don't know," I said, "but I hope to God it isn't me."

I took a left at the next corner. Normally, I would have pulled off the road and waited it out, but we had no time to waste. If we could just make it to the Vicious Turnpike, I could open it up and lose him. My compact Vesta was no match for the ten-cylinder engine of the Powercruiser that I was currently driving.

Suddenly, the Vesta shot out of a side road and came to a complete stop about twenty feet in front of us, blocking the road. Nyla screamed. I slammed on the brakes. The Powercruiser's tires locked in position as we squealed toward the Vesta. Whoever was in that car must have had a death wish. Either that, or he knew how well I could drive. The Powercruiser came to a complete stop just inches away from the passenger side door.

The Vesta's driver's side door opened up, and out stepped Martha. I breathed a sigh of relief. Of all the people who were gunning for me, Martha was by far the least worrisome.

She pulled a laser pistol out of her purse and began walking toward the Powercruiser, shakily holding the weapon out in front of her. I honked the horn and cracked my window. "Get out of the road!" I shouted out at her.

"Is that Martha?" Nyla asked.

"Either that or her ghost," I said. "She doesn't usually look this bad."

This is what's known in scholarly talk as an "understatement." Martha looked worse than a midget at a pedophile convention. Her makeup ran down her face sloppily, and not just the mascara—every bit of makeup on her face, from the eye shadow to the blush, looked like it was driving south for the winter. Atop her head, a scraggly mess of hair flowed into limp, tangled ringlets that brushed the top of a frayed, torn blouse. She looked like she'd spent the last day in a hurricane.

She fired a shot at the windshield. The beam ricocheted off the glass and into the sky.

"Laser pistols don't go through glass, honey," I shouted through the crack. "What the hell do you want? We're kinda pressed for time here."

Nyla chuckled.

"Was that a joke?" I asked, turning toward her.

"I don't know," she said. "Pressed for time ... to go back in time ... you could probably get something out of that."

"We're running out of time? Is that better?"

"Oh, yeah," Nyla said, nodding her head. "Because that's exactly what we're doing, we're running out of time. Running," making little running motions with her fingers, "out of time."

"Clever," I agreed.

Outside the windshield, Martha threw her gun down on the ground and collapsed.

"I guess I should get her out of the road," I said.

"Be careful," Nyla answered.

I opened the door and stepped out onto the street. Martha stretched out in a sobbing puddle on the road in front of me. I bent down, picked up the laser pistol, and tossed it through the window to Nyla for safekeeping.

I gently nudged Martha's quivering body with my foot. Funny how, when you finally let someone go, it's difficult to see them as a real person anymore. I felt like I was watching Martha on a telescreen. No sympathy, no empathy, not even the briefest spark of that old love that I once felt. She was nothing more to me than a roadblock on the way to my destination. And really, I was beginning to realize, that's all she had been for a long, long time.

"Hey," I said. "Hey, Martha. You have to get out of the road now."

Martha slowly crumpled her head in my direction and stared up into my face. Beneath the ghastly exterior, I could still see a glimmer of the dangerous beauty I once knew. It had only been 24 hours since I'd last seen her, but it felt like a lifetime, and looked like two.

"Johnny?" Martha asked. "Johnny, where am I?"

"You're lying in the middle of the street," I said. "And you look like hell."

Martha blinked and raised herself up on her elbow. I grabbed her arm and pulled her to her feet. She wobbled stupidly, like a baby taking its first steps.

"Come on now, Martha," I said. "We're gonna get you some help."

I walked her to the Vesta, opened the back door, and gently pushed her inside. She sprawled out across the backseat. I shut the door, walked over to the driver's seat, got in, backed the car over to the side of the road, and got back out.

"Help will be on its way any minute, Martha," I said. "Don't you worry."

"You know, Johnny," Martha said, wearily. "My only crime was loving you too much."

"That, and trying to kill me," I said. "Good-bye, Martha."

I slammed the door and walked back to the Powercruiser. In the sky, the sun had consumed half of the moon. We had no time to lose.

"Is she gonna be okay?" Nyla asked, as I settled behind the steering wheel.

"If by 'okay' you mean 'locked away in a loony bin for the rest of her life' then yeah, she's gonna be okay," I answered. "Now come on, Dolly Madison. We've got a lawn to rake."

27

From where I was sitting, it looked like life in Outer Borzoi was finally returning to normal. The line outside the Toilet was longer than usual, the result of an anxious city, ready to get back to its routine and ready to wax the floor with its wingtips and heels. It was a pleasing sight. Whatever ended up happening that night, I took some comfort in knowing that the disco community would be there to see me and Nyla perform the finest dance routine to ever grace the Toilet.

I pulled the Powercruiser into my usual spot and parked. Ten after nine. Twenty minutes early. Just enough time to slam a couple of shots of liquid confidence.

"What do you think, Johnny?" Nyla asked me.

"Trying not to, babe," I answered. "If someone else is pulling the strings, then I guess I'm just gonna try my damnedest to submit."

Nyla shook her head.

"You've got it all wrong, Johnny," she said. "We're the ones pulling the strings. Someone else just documented them. You've got all the freedom in the world. If you want to back out right now, you have all the power to do so."

"How can you say that for sure? If everything happens just as predicted, how can you argue for free will?" I asked.

"Because it wasn't predicted. It was recorded."

"But it hasn't happened yet," I countered.

"You're really a 'glass is half empty' kind of guy, aren't you?" she asked.

"Nah," I answered. "I would never leave a glass half empty. Anyway, Dolly, regardless of any philosophical baloney, I'm too deep in this one to walk away now. I gotta see how this ends."

"Me too," she answered.

"Me three," wrote Rory Carmichael.

Ever have that feeling that what you're about to do could change the course of your life? I'm not talking about that everyday feeling, when you have to choose between getting mayo on your sandwich or getting mustard; I'm talking about that enormous, atmospheric feeling, where the air around your body seems to pack you in tight and the outside world becomes your plaything. It's the feeling of ultimate control yet absolute powerlessness at the same time. Predictability goes out the window. You are split right down the middle—50% here, 50% there. You could play it safe, stick to what you know, and wait for the next cosmic fork to present itself in front of you. Or you could leap into the abyss and see what shimmies.

This is the essence of time travel. Time becomes bent at these junctures. Time stands still while it's moving forward. Everyone around you is going about their regular old lives, however fast or slow that may be, while you're traveling in a space-time journey through the now. Infinity stretches in front of you to either side. The past? Screw the past. It doesn't exist. The future, baby, that's where it's happening. Unless the future is the past, in which case, who knows?

Does free will exist? Is there such a thing as choice? These were the questions that I asked myself as we stood in front of the Toilet. Not consciously, mind you, not like, "Hey, Johnny Astronaut, does free will exist?" Words didn't come into play so much as panels, visions of a sort floating inside the endless space I called my brain. On a normal basis, I would weigh my options and the scale would tip in one direction or the other. But in this sort of situation, in which I was weighing the familiar unpleasantness against the unfamiliar possibilities, the scale cannot tip.

Normally, the past pushes you forward while the future pulls you ahead ... not now. Not in this moment. In this moment, or several moments, the future stops pulling. The past, it's always pushing. It's always disappearing right when you think you've got a handle on it. So you stand with your back against the wall of the past and let its momentum push you forward, until you get to that ultimate point, the moment when you must step away from the wall in one direction or the other. Now, whether the decision comes from within you or without you, I guess that's for faith to determine.

"What are you thinking about?" Nyla asked me.

"Existential dilemmas," I said.

"Come to any conclusions?" she asked.

"Yep," I replied. "Got it all sussed out. I solved the mystery of existence."

"Good," she said. "You'll have to explain it to me sometime."

"Read the book," I answered.

I could feel the eyes of the people in line upon us as we walked past the velvet ropes toward the front door. Nyla and I carried ourselves with the confidence of two people who were about to tear the dance floor into a million tiny pieces, and the people in line could sense it. Flames shot off of our bodies as we strolled, singeing the passersby into attention. Even Rascal, the doorman, was stunned. He let out a wolf whistle and shook his hand limply as we approached.

"Mama mia!" Rascal said. "Johnny Astronaut, you have got the spirit in you tonight! And what might this lovely young thing on your arm call herself?"

"I am Nyla," she said, offering her hand. Rascal lifted her hand to his lips and planted a gentle kiss upon it.

"You know," he said, under his breath, "some of my best friends are Ruskans."

"Glad to hear it, Rascal," I said. "You're a real stand-up guy."

"Hey, Johnny Astronaut," Rascal said jubilantly, "ain't no good can come of hate! You know what the song says ... love will keep us together."

"The other song says it'll tear us apart again," I answered. "But I'm willing to take my chances."

Rascal let out a jovial laugh and lifted the velvet rope to let us in.

"You're too much, Johnny Astronaut," he said. "Now get in there and teach these people some class."

We walked through the front door and into the bustling discotheque. Over the speakers, a solid gold remix of Peaches and Herb tickled the club-goers into a frenzy of whirling arms and legs. I looked at Nyla. Gazing upon her face, lit magnificently with a pure smile of happiness and expectation, I felt a rush of pride. This was my lady, this was my place, and this was my night.

We looked over to the bar, where Henry was spinning out drinks like a cocktail tornado. He glanced up from his mixing and nodded at me. I nodded back. We crossed the crowded dance floor and squeezed our way up to the bar. He finished filling his order and walked to where we were standing.

"Everything's in place," he said, as quietly as he could manage in the boisterous disco atmosphere. "The boys are up in the DJ booth, awaiting the signal. I'm going to give you a minute or two to compose yourselves and think about the steps. Whenever you're ready, I want you to walk out to the floor and clap your hands. And then ... do what you do, and do it well. We've only got one shot at this. Let's shoot to kill."

Nyla began shivering next to me. Henry smiled hopefully and placed his hand on hers. I put my arm around her shoulder.

"What's the matter, baby?" I asked. "You need a drink?"

"No," she answered, quietly sobbing under her breath, "I'm just nervous, is all."

"Well, nuts," I said, "stop worrying. We know it's gonna turn out okay. It's all in the book, right Henry?"

Henry nodded. "It's all in the book."

"What does the book say about me getting a little drink before I hit the dance floor?" I asked him.

"No way, Johnny," Nyla sniffled. "There'll be plenty of time for drinking when we hit the 21st century. Right now, you've gotta stay sharp."

I grimaced. No one told me I was signing up for the non-alcoholic cruise. In the interest of universe preservation, though, I bit my tongue. And then I bit it a little harder, thinking that maybe there was a little bit of alcohol soaked up inside that thing that I could release. No such luck. Apparently tongues don't work that way.

Beneath my arm, Nyla was shaking with tears. The people surrounding us pitched us dirty glances. No one likes a sobbing woman in a bar, especially when that woman is preventing them from getting their drinks.

"Thank you, Henry," Nyla squeaked through her tears. "I will miss you forever."

"I'll miss you, too, baby," Henry replied. "Make me proud."

"I don't really know you," I said to him. "But thanks for the smokes."

Henry winked. "You betcha."

The patrons around us were starting to grumble. "Get a room, you three," shouted some guy, to mild chuckles. "Get me a beer, first," answered another guy, to milder chuckles.

"Good luck," Henry mouthed, before returning to his duties behind the bar.

I looked into Nyla's eyes, which were red and puffy from crying.

"Look, we're gonna do great, kiddo," I said.

"I know," she answered. "I'm just worried about what's going to happen to everyone after we ... you know."

"Where we're going, they don't exist yet," I said. "So put that thought out of your head."

"Where we're going, we don't exist yet," she said.

"Good point," I acknowledged. "At any rate, there's no turning back now, dollface. So I say we go shake a tail feather while the getting's good."

She raised her head and looked into my eyes. I could feel my body melting into a puddle at her feet. She threw her arm behind my neck and gently pulled my head down to hers, planting a warm, delicate kiss upon my lips. "Good luck, Johnny," she whispered in my ear. "Good destiny," I whispered back.

Nyla grabbed my hand and led me out to the center of the dance floor. As we brushed through the crowd, the other dancers stared and whispered to each other. "That's Johnny Astronaut," I heard one of them say. "He's the best." They knew what to do. If they didn't let the captain have his room, this ship was gonna sink. Nyla and I clapped, per Henry's instructions.

On cue, a loud scratch shot out of the speakers, interrupting "Dancing Queen." The room went deathly quiet. Nyla and I quickly got into position. I pointed my right leg out to the side and my left arm up in the air. Nyla mirrored my position to the left. The crowd around us noticed what we were doing and backed away, giving us an open dance floor all to ourselves.

In the silence, I heard a familiar hiss wafting out of the crowd in front of me.

"Assssstronaut."

From the middle of the tightly packed crowd, the Ptsaurians began shoving their way to the front. My pulse began to race. This was just what we needed. I swung my neck around to the right and caught Henry's eyes. "Go on," he mouthed.

Suddenly, the front door swung open, loudly. Charvez stepped into the doorframe, surrounded by his goons from Central D.

"Johnny Astronaut," he said, staring across the dance floor at me, still in position. "I have a warrant for your arrest."

Just then, the needle dropped, and the opening beats of "Whistle Bump" filled the air. A cheer arose from the crowd. I looked at Nyla with a pleading expression.

"Whatever you do," she said. "Don't stop dancing."

I nodded.

"Yarrrrgh!"

A fierce cry rang out from the second floor, followed by the sound of breaking glass. We looked up to see the four Ruskans break through the glass of the DJ booth and leap into the crowd, directly onto the shoulders of the Ptsaurians. The Ptsaurians hissed and swung their bodies around, desperately trying to shake the Ruskans. At the front door, Charvez stood, enraptured by the melee that was beginning to take place in front of him. To our right, Henry leapt over the bar and began making his way to Charvez.

The first bar after the intro kicked in, and the dance began. Nyla and I launched into alternating bounce steps. I felt tight, nervous. Nyla could tell. I swung her into my body and wrapped my arms around hers.

"It's all in the book," she whispered. "we get out of here alive, and I'll let you fuck me up the ass."

"Watch your mouth, dame," I said. "And watch my fucking feet."

I spun her out and released. Charvez began making his move to the dance floor. The crowd around us surged and broiled like a sea about to burst as the spectators surrounding the Ptsaurians and Ruskans got swept into the flood of violence. And I was just getting warmed up.

Behind me, Nyla was working the remaining crowd members with a tight Pigeon Step. I started into the solo section with gusto. A Cross Step flowed into a New York Hustle, followed by a Bus Stop, then back to a New York Hustle. My pulse finally locked into the beat, and the song began to lift my feet off the dance floor. If the spectators weren't already hooked or rioting, they were by the time I finished this combination.

Out of the corner of my eye, I saw Charvez pull his gun. Henry made a flying leap and tackled Charvez into a group of people, sending drinks and hats into the air. The patrons at the bar took this as their cue to start smashing bottles and glasses and chugging beer right out of the tap. Charvez's goons barked orders at a crowd that paid them no mind.

Nyla Cross Stepped up to my side. I joined in on the second beat. The crowd applauded and shouted death threats at one another. I spun her in, then out, then in, then between my legs, up into the air, then onto my left shoulder, over the head, right shoulder, then back on the ground in precise rhythm. Around us, the room pulsed with angry energy. Ruskans fought Petruskans. Ptsaurians fought them both. Tiberinians and Paraderms and Fesdins and Terramorphs all joined in the fray, until the entire place was in the spread, save for me and Nyla, still dancing at the center of the floor.

Nyla stepped out for her solo, as I took up the Pigeon Step behind her. She leapt into the air and spun around, landing in a perfect split, then bouncing back up on the second beat and snapping a quick Kick Leap followed by a Hand Spring. I had never felt so alive, so in tune, so in touch, so out of touch. The air was quivering. No, shaking. No, bending, actually bending in front of my eyes. I could see the rift, slicing Nyla's body in two. I reached my hand out to her and pulled her into my body.

"Do you feel that?" I asked her. "It's starting."

"I know," she said. "We're almost done."

A shot rang out in the future, or maybe it was the past ... and then I heard it again. I looked through the widening time hole in front of me to see Charvez shoot Henry, then shoot him again, then the Ruskans jumped out of the DJ booth, Henry collapsed, uncollapsed, collapsed again. Nyla screamed, but no sound carried, even though I remembered hearing it. We couldn't stop now; it had begun, and we were powerless to stop it. Nyla swung out to my side and prepped to begin the final, most challenging groove in our routine—The Sling Hustle.

The beat was getting slower. I felt like I was hustling in water. Nyla hustled next to me, still perfectly in sync, in spite of the cooler tempo. To the left. To the right. Front. Back. Side to side. And then a turn in place, and a leap. As we leapt, the room began to spin out of control. I had only Nyla to mark my position, and she only me.

Voices slipped out of the time hole and hung in the air in front of me like words on a giant screen. The Sifter? Who was the Sifter? I was suddenly flooded with memories that didn't seem to belong to me ... a man with blue hair, a psychologist, a boy with a giant lollipop. An insatiable craving for Coney dogs. What the hell was a Coney dog?

We were almost finished. All we needed now was to hit the final freeze. For what seemed to be the next several minutes, Nyla bounded away from me. I waited, steady as a rock amidst the turmoil surrounding us. The voices continued building, echoes from a past that I didn't remember but couldn't forget.

When Nyla finally came, she came like fire, blazing across the dance floor into my open arms. I held my arms rigidly in front of me and caught her, snap, in mid-air. Across the floor, Charvez stood up and lifted his gun into the air. A flash of smoke flew out of the barrel. I could see the bullet approaching, slowly, flying through the air in no particular hurry. It penetrated the air in front of us and hung there, stuck in eternal jelly, awaiting further instructions.

As the bullet watched menacingly, I spun around, flipped Nyla into the air, pulled her down my body, until she finally came to rest, one hand and leg on the floor, in our final

Freeze.

1

The asshole who lives next door to me won't stop sifting his lawn.

We've almost come to blows several times about this little idiosyncrasy. I can't stand to watch it. Every time I go outside, there he is with his asshole rake, running the forked end through his tall grass. I suggested to him once that if he was so concerned about the appearance of his lawn, he really should try to mow every once in awhile. He just shrugged me off. I've begun to suspect that he sees his sifting as having some kind of social importance, as though he's working his rake for the little guy, the guy who has no rake of his own. "I don't have a rake," I said to him once. "Are you raking for me?"

"No," he replied, affirmatively. It was an affirmative negative.

I didn't pry beyond that. I can't argue with double negatives, especially when one of them is positive.

I have spoken with my analyst, Dr. Brody, about the Sifter several times. She doesn't understand what the big deal is. I told her that I couldn't relax with that bastard sifting his lawn all the time.

"Just ignore him," she said. "What effect does it have on you if he's sifting? It's not like he's sifting your lawn."

"But don't you see?" I asked, flabbergasted. "He might as well be sifting my lawn. He seems to think he's sifting the lawn of the common man. In fact, were he sifting my lawn, I could see the nobility in his actions. I would say, 'Hey, buddy, thanks for sifting, you're doing the Lord's work.' But no. He wants to claim credit for things he hasn't done, and I, for one, don't cotton to that sort of behavior."

Dr. Brody thinks I'm crazy. I know that because I have asked her on several occasions.

"Do you think I'm crazy?" I asked her one day, shortly before her husband died.

"Yes," she said, nodding vigorously. "Vehemently."

"I don't think you can use vehemently in that manner," I said.

"What do you mean?" she asked. "Of course I can. It denotes emphasis."

"But only in a certain manner," I replied. "You can say that you agree vehemently. But you can't say 'yes' vehemently. The word doesn't work that way."

Dr. Brody threw up her hands in frustration.

"You are vehemently frustrated with me," I noted.

Sometimes I think that everything would be better for Dr. Brody if she could just get laid more often. She loves to talk about sex. Before Dr. Brody, I went to another analyst who also loved to talk about sex. I started to develop a theory about how analysts were obsessed with sex, but then I began to worry that it was my problem. Maybe in the same way that one tends to date the same sort of woman over and over again, one chooses the same sort of analyst. It's not conscious. From the first meeting, the women seem to be entirely different creatures. And you convince yourself, 'The others, they all shared a similar fault. This one, she's different.' But then two months later, it's the same old bullshit.

Could be too, though, that I'm just constructing the patterns in these women through my own behavior, that they're actually the ones responding to me. I guess it all comes down to the choice between free will and destiny, as most things do.

Dr. Brody doesn't believe in free will. She thinks that all of our actions and thoughts are controlled by some complex set of chemical reactions, or should I say, her chemical reactions inform her that all of our thoughts and actions are controlled by some complex set of chemical reactions. We got into a rather heated argument about it this morning. It seems like most of my arguments with Dr. Brody become heated. I think it's because she's passionate for me. She disagrees. She says she's passionate about helping people. I suggested that her insistence on constantly referring to me as "fat ass" was not very helpful. She claimed it was tough love.

"How can you not believe in free will? Do you know something I don't?" I asked her at this morning's session.

"Why must you always argue with me?" she asked.

"Did someone else choose that question for you?" I demanded. "Who's pulling the strings, Brody? WHO'S PULLING THE STRINGS?"

Dr. Brody rolled her eyes. Sometimes I think she doesn't take me very seriously.

"Can we talk about erectile dysfunction?" she asked.

That's another thing about Dr. Brody; she loves to talk about erections. She comes from some weird school that believes everything boils down to sex. I think it's all bullshit. Sometimes I don't know if she's helping me or if I'm helping her.

Dr. Brody's husband died of cancer not too long ago. There's nothing funny about this. For months, he struggled along, until it got so bad that he couldn't even drink fluids. Can you imagine? The whole experience had a very negative effect on Dr. Brody. For months, I would come into my sessions to find her sitting at her desk, crying. I once told her that this was not very professional behavior, and she threw a clipboard at me. It's not that I didn't empathize. I was putting myself in the shoes of someone who had never visited her before. In the business world, you have to sell, sell, sell, and a sobbing psychotherapist is not a very good advertisement for the healing powers of psychotherapy. If I walked into a normal doctor's office and saw the doctor hitting himself in the head with a hammer, I might be inclined to leave.

This morning we talked about her husband's death a little bit. She really opened up to me. She told me that at the end there, she just wanted him to die. I suggested that maybe she really wanted him to die all along and she threw me out of the office. It was a very productive session.

I was on such a successful healing spree that I decided to visit my psychic afterwards. My psychic and Dr. Brody are in love, but neither of them knows it yet. I'm waiting for the proper moment to broach the subject with Dr. Brody. I was going to bring it up a little while ago, but my psychic suggested that I should give her some time to heal. I wonder how much time it takes someone to heal after a death? I think I'm being very patient. It's been almost three weeks now. But if there's one thing my psychic understands, it's human behavior, and he has told me that now is not the time.

"So ... when do you want me to introduce you to Dr. Brody?" I asked him at the beginning of today's session.

He smiled benevolently.

"All things in due time, my friend," he said. "The story of life is writ large. All things in due time."

"I don't understand what you're talking about," I said.

Dr. Brody and my psychic would be perfect for each other because they are diametrically opposed. She believes in the mind and he believes in the spirit. I can't think of a better match. They might loathe one another, but their children would be very well rounded.

Dr. Brody has gotten a head start on the relationship by choosing to hate my psychic before she's even met him. She thinks that psychic powers are baloney. I used to think that he hated her, but I've come to the conclusion in recent months that my psychic doesn't have much of an opinion about things. He's one of those "everything is beautiful, yet everything is ugly," kind of people. There's no use in arguing with that sort, because they agree and disagree with everything you have to say. I still get a kick out of him, though, and I think I've really been making a lot of progress in my telekinetic abilities.

A few months back, my psychic started telling me that I was going to meet a mysterious person who would change the course of my life. I feel like every day I meet mysterious people, but according to him, I have not yet met the mysterious person to whom he was referring. "Look," I said to him, "every day I come here and tell you about some person I met who makes no freaking sense. What qualifies someone as mysterious?"

"I don't know," he said, "but I would know if you met the person I'm thinking about, and you haven't."

"Can you give me more details?" I asked. "It's really driving me crazy. I feel like I'm suspicious of everyone, all the time."

"You have always been suspicious of everyone, all the time," he answered. "It's in your nature."

It is, too. If people made more sense, I would have no reason to be suspicious of their motives, but they don't, so I am. The other day I went into Angelo's to get a Coney dog and the kid who waited on me had blue hair. Blue hair! Can you imagine?

"You must've done something really bad for your parents to make you get your hair dyed that color," I said.

He glowered at me. That's the only word I can use for it, he glowered. I wouldn't give in, though. Sometimes I don't know when to shut up.

"What are you trying prove by dying your hair like that?" I asked.

"Not trying to prove nothin'," he said. "It looks cool."

"Well, then, you're trying to prove that it looks cool," I answered.

"Nuh-uh," he protested. "Why can't I just dye my hair this color because I feel like it? They sell the color for a reason, and that reason is because people sometimes feel like dying their hair this color. Just because you don't have any hair is no reason to judge those who do."

"Can I have my Coney dog?" I asked him, bored with the conversation.

I told my psychic about this interaction and he seemed amused. He was amused because he can't see the horrible truth behind the conversation: the whole world has gone screwy. When dying your hair blue is such an accepted phenomenon that they let the kid with the blue hair serve you your Coney dog, things have gone screwy beyond repair. What's next? Am I going to have to order my sandwich from a guy with an ape head grafted onto his body? At the bank, would I be comfortable giving my deposit to a woman with two extra eyes installed in her cheeks? The future is more terrifying than any of us can imagine.

Human engineering, they call it. I say it's bunko.

"Bunko!" I shouted at my psychic.

"Relax," he said. "I have good news for you."

My ears perked up. They didn't literally perk up. Someday, maybe they'll human-engineer ears to perk up so that we can be more confident in our descriptions.

"I could use some good news," I said. "It seems like all I've been hearing lately are dire predictions. One can only take so many dire predictions before one becomes dire oneself, and I like to pride myself on my positive outlook."

"The good news is this," he said, ignoring my digression. "Today, you will finally meet the mysterious stranger."

"That is good news," I agreed. "Where am I going to meet him?"

"I can't tell you that," he said.

"You're the worst psychic I've ever known," I answered.

He smiled benevolently, at peace with his abilities. Like I said, with some people, you just can't argue.

On the walk home, I glared at everyone I passed with suspicious eyes. I got a few funny looks, but mostly people minded their own business. If they wanted to write me off as crazy, that was their prerogative. I'm sure they had a few screws loose themselves.

A few houses away from my own, I froze in my tracks. Coming towards me was my arch-nemesis, the Little Sailor Boy. He's this kid who lives down the block from me. His mother dresses him in these queer little sailor suits. He's always licking an enormous lollipop. I am filled with indescribable hatred for this little monster. He's never done anything to me, unless you consider that his existence is a blight on my own.

Today he was walking without his mother. I didn't think that was very safe, especially with rage-filled lunatics like myself prowling the streets. Thankfully, I had not yet traveled so far down the waterslide of sanity that I was unable to control myself. I knew that I could get into quite a bit of trouble if I let my rage become known to the kid. I had already had a run-in with him in the bathroom at Angelo's of which I was not entirely proud.

I picked up the pace and shot past him, past the Sifter, straight to my front door. That was close. I reminded myself that I probably shouldn't spend much time outside the house.

I've been spending a lot of time in my basement lately. It's filthy, but it makes me comfortable. I've been trying to get some writing done, and there are too many distractions upstairs. Down in the basement, I can concentrate. Trouble is, as of late, I've had nothing to concentrate on.

I sat down at my desk and turned on my computer. I love that word, "my." I looked around the basement at all of the things I could rightfully designate as mine. There was quite a bit. The broken TV. The piles of things I'd found in other people's garbage. I owned a lot, all right. Mine was quite a successful life.

While I was waiting for my computer to boot up, the doorbell rang. I wasn't aware that my doorbell even worked, but there it was, ringing. I thought about my psychic's prediction. Could this be the mysterious stranger? I stood up from my chair and looked out the basement window to see two pairs of legs standing on my front porch. Two pairs. One person going around ringing people's doorbells is a mysterious stranger; two people are a conspiracy. I decided I best not take any chances. I grabbed a broken broom handle from one of the piles of my stuff and headed up the stairs to the front room.

I flung the door open, just as the pair was reaching to ring the bell again. They reeled back in surprise at the sudden response. Good.

"What do you want from me?" I bellowed in a terrifying voice, shaking my whapping stick.

Standing on my porch was an attractive young couple. Cultists, I would imagine. They looked like something straight out of a forties' crime movie, and slightly self-consciously so, as though they had woken up this morning and decided to play detective. The man was wearing a three-piece suit with a Fedora perched just atop his eyes. The woman, quite attractive, wore a low-cut dress that revealed a striking figure. She had wide, beautiful eyes that made me feel a little giddy. I chose to direct my conversation at the man.

"What?" I asked again, sternly.

"Pleased to meet you, pops," the man said. "I'm Johnny Astronaut, and this is my girl, Nyla."

"And I'm Rory Truckdriver," I said. "What do you want from me?"

"We need your help," Johnny said. "You've got something we need, locked away in that big ol' brain of yours. You wanna know what we're looking for? You're gonna have to invite us in, first."

I didn't like the sound of that. I clutched my broomstick and raised it into a possible defense position.

"You're not going to suck my brain out, are you?" I asked, cautiously.

The two looked at each other and burst into laughter.

"No, pal, that's not our speed," Johnny chuckled. "We just want to have a little conversation, see? Nice and friendly."

Nyla smiled and batted her eyelashes coyly. She was his secret weapon. Without her, I would have slammed the door in this wacko's face ... but I couldn't resist a beautiful pair of eyes. Great tits, too. I opened the door and led them into the living room.

"Swell place you got here, bub," Astronaut said. "I hear the dank cavern look is quite in vogue this year."

He and Nyla sat down on my couch. Johnny propped his legs up on the coffee table. Nyla coolly surveyed the room. I dropped into the chair next to the couch, still clutching my broom handle, in case things got feisty.

"What do you want?" I asked, tersely.

Johnny Astronaut removed his legs from the coffee table and set them on the floor.

"We need you to write a book for us," he said.

"Sorry, brother," I replied. "I don't write on demand."

"But you gotta," Johnny said. "The fabric of the universe depends on it."

"Oh yeah?" I asked. "The universe wants me to write your book? You can tell the universe to take a flying leap. I'm not interested."

"We come from the future," Nyla interjected.

I nodded. "I suspected as much."

Over the course of the next few hours, Johnny and Nyla told me their story. I tried to listen attentively, but truth be told, I lost my concentration from time to time. It's hard to pay attention to a several-hour story. I can't even pay attention to a two-hour movie. I start thinking about all of the other directions the script could have taken and I get upset when I see that it's just the same old mind-numbing crap, over and over again. People like to predict things, like babies playing peek-a-boo. You throw 'em a curveball and they get mad at you.

"... and the next thing we knew, we were standing in a cornfield in Idaho. Since then, we've been seeking you out. We've had a helluva time tracking you down. No one seems to know who you are."

It had gotten dark since they began talking. I wanted to get them out before it got much later. I didn't know if they had a place to stay, and I wouldn't be able to sleep comfortably with an insane couple on my couch.

"That's a great story," I agreed, nodding my head like an idiot. "I'm going to get downstairs and start writing it right away."

Johnny and Nyla looked at each other and smiled tenderly. We sat that way in silence for an uncomfortable amount of time, nodding and smiling, smiling and nodding.

"I think you should leave now," I finally said.

They turned to me and grinned. Johnny flung out his hand.

"Thanks, partner," he said. "Can't wait to read it."

I shook his hand enthusiastically.

"All right, good-bye now," I said, shuttering them toward the door.

They paused at the doorway.

"Oh, one more thing, pops," Johnny began. "Do you know of any good discos around here?"

"Discos?" I asked. "Try 1978."

They stared at me, perplexed, then looked at each other, shrugged their shoulders, and took off down the driveway. The neighbor was still sifting his lawn. He waved to them as they walked by, perhaps recognizing a couple of kindred idiots.

I closed the door and locked it behind me, then went back down to the basement and sat at my typewriter. What to write about? Nothing interesting ever happened to me. I looked out the window. Johnny and Nyla receded in the distance, while the Sifter went about his business, combing through his overgrown lawn. Maybe he was looking for something.

What a bunch of bull crap. Why must people make my life so difficult? 'All right,' I finally decided, 'they want me to write a story? I'll write a story. Can't escape the narrative? I'll give you narrative. I'll take your crap story and turn it into gold. We'll see about the universe exploding when I get through with it.'

Some of the details would have to be changed, of course, to make it more exciting. From inside, everyone's life seems like a bucket of chuckles, but then when you put it down on paper, it's just a bunch of bullshit with some in-jokes tossed in for annoyance.

I cracked my knuckles and began writing:

"Next stop, Outer Borzoi."

Fuck literature.

www.contemporarypress.com

Current Titles

Dead Dog by Mike Segretto: A curmudgeonly shut-in's life is turned inside-out when he becomes involved with a trash-talking femme fatale, a trio of psychotic gangsters, and a dog whose incessant barking has caused him years of sleepless nights. Spiked with ample doses of sex, violence and campy humor, Dead Dog is a riotous road trip from an Arizona trailer park to hell.
ISBN 0-9744614-0-7

Down Girl by Jess Dukes: In Down Girl, 29-year-old Pauline Rose Lennon works too hard for every cent she ever made until she meets Anton, willing to give her more cash than she's ever imagined...for one small favor. Pauline's life spins hilariously out of control, but she pulls it back from the brink just in time to prove that just because you're down, it doesn't mean you're out.
ISBN 0-9744614-1-5

Wet Work by Jay Brida: Wet Work is a story of lusty agents turned on by violence, lazy detectives on the take and drug-abusing Russians looking to kill American leaders. And those are the good guys. With memorable characters, zinging dialogue and a sexy, twisting plot, Wet Work takes on all comers and mops up the floor with them.
ISBN 0-9744614-2-3

Upcoming Titles

G.O.P D.O.A by Jay Brida

Skin Slips by Charles Nickles

VIII going on IX by Dennis Hayes

CP

contemporary press

Contemporary Press (est. 2003) is committed to truth, justice and going our own way. When Big Publishing dies, we're the cockroaches who will devour their bones and dance on their graves.